THE CRIME DOCTOR

BY

ERNEST W. HORNUNG

With Illustrations by
FREDERIC DORR STEELE

British Library Cataloguing-in-Publication Data
A catalogue record for this book is available from the
British Library

"It was struck with—this"

Contents

E. W. Hornung

Ernest William Hornung was born in Middlesbrough, England in 1866. He spent most of his youth in England and France, but had a two-year stay in Australia during his teens which greatly influenced much of his later work. In 1893, having returned to England, Hornung married Constance Aimée Monica Doyle, the sister of his friend and great author Arthur Conan Doyle. After working briefly as a journalist, and publishing a series of poems in *The Times,* Hornung created the character for which he is best-remembered: A. J. Raffles, a "gentleman thief" plying his trade in Victorian London. Raffles first appeared in 1898, and went on to star in a string of stories and a full-length novel, *Mr. Justice Raffles* (1909). Hornung also wrote on the subject of cricket, and was a skilled player of the sport. In 1915, his only son was killed at Ypres; in response, Hornung took up work with the YMCA in France, dying six years later, in 1921.

I

THE PHYSICIAN WHO HEALED HIMSELF

In the course of his meteoric career as Secretary of State for the Home Department, the Right Honorable Topham Vinson instituted many reforms and earned the reformer's whack of praise and blame. His methods were not those of the permanent staff; and while his notorious courage endeared him to the young, it was not in so strong a nature to leave friend or foe lukewarm. An assiduous contempt for tradition fanned the flame of either faction, besides leading to several of those personal adventures which were as breath to the Minister's unregenerate nostrils, but which never came out without exposing him to almost universal censure. It is matter for thanksgiving that the majority of his indiscretions were unguessed while he and his held office; for he was never so unconventional as in pursuance of those enlightened tactics on which his reputation rests, or in the company of that kindred spirit who had so much to do with their inception.

It was early in an autumn session that this remarkable pair became acquainted. Mr. Vinson had been tempted by the mildness of the night to walk back from Westminster to Portman Square. He had just reached home when he heard his name cried from some little distance behind him. The voice tempered hoarse excitement with the restraint due to midnight in a quiet square; and as Mr. Vinson turned on his door-step, a young man rushed across the road with a gold chain swinging from his outstretched hand.

"Your watch, sir, your watch!" he gasped, and displayed a bulbous hunter with a monogram on one side and the crest of all the Vinsons on the other.

"Heavens!" cried the Home Secretary, feeling in an empty waistcoat pocket before he could believe his eyes. "Where on earth did you find that? I had it on me when I left the House."

"It wasn't a case of findings," said the young man, as he fanned himself with his opera hat. "I've just taken it from the fellow who took it from you."

"Who? Where?" demanded the Secretary of State, with unstatesmanlike excitement.

"Some poor brute in North Audley Street, I think it was."

"That's it! That was where he stopped me, just at the corner of Grosvenor Square!" exclaimed Vinson. "And I went and gave the old scoundrel half-a-crown!"

"He probably had your watch while you were looking in your purse."

And the young man dabbed a very good forehead, that glistened in the light from the open door, with a white silk handkerchief just extracted from his sleeve.

"But where were you?" asked Topham Vinson, taking in every inch of him.

"I'd just come into the square myself. You had just gone out of it. The pickpocket was looking to see what he'd got, even while he hurled his blessings after you."

"And where is he now? Did he slip through your fingers?"

"I'm ashamed to say he did; but your watch didn't!" its owner was reminded with more spirit. "I could guess whose it was by the crest and monogram, and I decided to make sure instead of giving chase."

"You did admirably," declared the Home Secretary, in belated appreciation. "I'm in the papers quite enough without appearing as a mug out of office hours. Come in, please, and let me thank you with all the honors possible at this time of night."

And, taking him by the arm, he ushered the savior of his property into a charming inner hall, where elaborate refreshments stood in readiness on a side-table, and a bright fire looked as acceptable as the saddlebag chairs drawn up beside it. A bottle and a pint of reputable champagne had been left out with the oysters and the caviar; and Mr. Vinson, explaining that he never allowed anybody to sit up for him, opened the bottle with the precision of a practised hand, and led the attack on food and drink with schoolboy gusto and high spirits.

In the meantime there had been some mutual note-taking. The Home Secretary, whose emphatic personality lent itself to the discreet pencil of the modern caricaturist, was in appearance exactly as represented in contemporary cartoons; there was nothing unexpected about him, since his boyish vivacity was a quality already over-exploited by the Press. His frankness was something qualified by a gaze of habitual penetration, but still it was there, and his manner could evidently be grand or colloquial at will. The surprise was in his surroundings rather than in the man himself. The perfect union of luxury and taste is none too common in the professed Sybarite who is that and nothing more; in men of action and pugnacious politicians it is yet another sign of sheer capacity. The bits of rich old furniture, the old glass twinkling at every facet, the brasses blazing in the firelight, the few but fine prints on the Morris wallpaper, might have won the approval of an art student, and the creature comforts that of the youngest epicure.

The young man from the street was easily pleased in all such respects; but indoors he no longer looked quite the young man. He had taken off an overcoat while his host was opening the champagne, and evening clothes accentuated a mature gauntness of body and limb. His hair, which was dark and wiry, was beginning to bleach at the temples; and up above one ear there was a little disk of downright silver, like a new florin. The shaven face was pale, eager, and austere. Dark eyes burnt like beacons under a noble brow, and did not lose in character or intensity by a distinct though slight strabism. So at least it seemed to Topham Vinson, who was a really wonderful judge of faces, yet had seldom seen one harder to sum up.

"I'm sorry you don't smoke," said he, snipping a cigar which he had extolled in vain. "And that champagne, you know! You haven't touched it, and you really should."

The other was on his legs that instant. "I never smoke and seldom drink," he exclaimed; "but I simply can not endure your hospitality, kind as it is, Mr. Vinson, without being a bit more honest with you than I've been so far. I didn't lose that pickpocket by accident or because he was too quick for me. I—I purposely packed him off."

In the depths of his softest chair Mr. Vinson lolled smiling—but not with his upturned eyes. They were the steel eyes of all his tribe, but trebly keen, as became its intellectual head and chief.

"The fellow pitched a pathetic yarn?" he conjectured. He had never seen a more miserable specimen, he was bound to say.

"It wasn't that, Mr. Vinson. I should have let him go in any case—once I'd recovered what he'd taken—as a matter of principle."

"Principle!" cried the Secretary of State. But he did not modify his front-bench attitude; it was only the well-known eyebrows that rose.

"The whole thing is," his guest continued, yet more frankly, "that I happen to hold my own views on crime and its punishment If I might be permitted to explain them, however briefly, they would at least afford the only excuse I have to offer for my conduct. If you consider it no excuse, and if I have put myself within reach of the law, there, sir, is my card; and here am I, prepared to take the consequences of my act."

The Home Secretary leaned forward and took the card from a sensitive hand, vibrant as the voice to which he had just been listening, but no more tremulous. Again he looked up, into a pale face grown paler still, and dark eyes smoldering with suppressed enthusiasm. It was by no means his baptism of that sort of fire; but it seemed to Mr. Vinson that here was a new type of eccentric zealot; and it was only by an effort that he resumed his House of Commons attitude and his smile.

"I see, Doctor Dollar, that you are a near neighbor of mine—only just round the corner in Welbeck Street. May I take it that your experience as a consultant is the basis of the views you mention?"

"My experience as an alienist," said Doctor Dollar, "so far as I can lay claims to that euphemism."

"And how far is that, doctor?"

"In the sense that all crime is a form of madness."

"Then you would call yourself——"

The broken sentence ended on a note as tactfully remote from the direct interrogative as practised speech could make it.

"In default of a recognized term," said Doctor Dollar, "which time will confer as part of a wider recognition, I can only call myself a crime doctor."

"A branch not yet acknowledged by your profession?"

"Neither by my profession nor by the law, Mr. Vinson; but both have got to come to it, just as surely as we all accept the other scientific developments of the day."

"But have you reduced your practise to a science, doctor?"

"I am doing so," said Doctor Dollar, with the restrained confidence which could not but impress one who knew the value of that quality in himself and in others. "I have made a start; if it were not so late I would tell you all about it. You are the Home Secretary of England, the man of all others whom I could wish to convert to my views. But already

I have kept you up too long. If you would grant me an appointment——"

"Not at all," interrupted Mr. Vinson, as he settled himself even more comfortably in his chair. "The night is still young—so is my cigar. Pray say all you care to say, and say it as confidentially as you please. You interest me, Doctor Dollar; nor can I forget that I am much indebted to you."

"I don't want to trade on that," returned the doctor, hastily. "But it is an old dream of mine to tell you, sir, about my work, and how and why I came to take it up. I was not intended for medicine, you see; my people are army people, were Border outlaws once upon a time, and fighting folk ever since. My father was an ensign in the Crimea—Scots Fusiliers. I joined the Argyll and Sutherlands the year before South Africa—where, by the way, I remember seeing you with your Yeomen."

"I had eighteen months of it without a headache or a scratch."

"I wish I could say the same, Mr. Vinson. I was shot through the head at the Modder, ten days after I landed."

"Through the head, did you say?" asked the Home Secretary, lifting his own some inches.

The doctor touched the silver patch in his dark strong hair. "That's where the bullet came slinking out; any but a Mauser would have carried all before it! As it was, it left me with a bit of a squint, as you can see; otherwise, in a very few weeks, I was as fit as ever—physically."

"Wonderful!"

"Physically and even mentally—from a medical point of view—but not morally, Mr. Vinson! Something subtle had happened, some pressure somewhere, some form of local paralysis. And it left me a pretty low-down type, I can tell you! It was a case of absolute automatism—but I won't go into particulars now, if you don't mind."

"On no account, my dear doctor!" exclaimed the Secretary of State, with inadvertent cordiality. "This is all of extraordinary interest. I believe I can see what's coming. But I want to hear every word you care to tell me—and not one that you don't."

"It had destroyed my moral sense on just one curious point; but, thank God, I came to see the cause as well as to suffer unspeakably from the effect. After that it was a case of killing or curing oneself by hook or by crook. I decided to try the curing first. And—to cut a long yarn short—I *was* cured."

"Easily?"

"No. The slander may come home to roost, but I shall never think much of the London specialist! I've dropped my two sovereigns and a florin into too many of their itching palms, beginning with the baronets and knights and ending up with the unknown adventures. But not a man-Jack of them was ashamed to pocket his two guineas (in one case three) for politely telling me I was as mad as a hatter to think of such a thing as really was the matter with me!"

"And in the end?"

"In the end I struck a fellow with an open mind—but not in England—and if I said that he literally opened mine it might be an exaggeration, but that's all. He did go prospecting in my skull—risked his reputation as against my life—but we both came out on top."

"And you've been your own man ever since?"

Topham Vinson asked the question gravely; it would have taken as keen a superficial observer as himself to detect much difference in his manner, in his eyes, in anything about him. Doctor Dollar was not that kind of observer. To see far one must look high, and to look high is to miss things under one's nose. It is all a matter of mental trajectory. In the sheer height of his enthusiasm, the soaring visionary was losing touch with the hard-headed groundling in the chair.

"I was cured," he answered with tense simplicity. "It was a miraculous cure, and yet no miracle. Anybody could perform its like, given the nerve and skill. Yet it seemed to me a new thing; its possibilities were almost appalling in their fascination. I must not speak of them, for in a large measure they are only possibilities still. But I resolved to qualify, so that at least I might be in a position to do as I had been done by. I had already left the service; but my fighting days were not over. I was going to fight Crime as it had never been fought before!"

There was a challenge in the pause made here. But the listener did not take it up, and the harangue ended on a humbler note:

"I studied at St. Mary's under men whose names you know as well as they know yours. I was at Berlin under Winterschladen, and with Jens Jennsen in Stockholm. Before I was thirty I had put up my plate in Welbeck Street, and there I am still."

"And yet," said the Home Secretary, with a faint and wary smile—"and yet the possibilities are still only possibilities!"

"On the surgical side, yes; there I was misled by my own abnormal case. When another sudden injury makes a monkey of an honest man, I know where to take him; but the average injury is too gradual, too subtle for the knife. Congenital cases are, of course, quite hopeless in that respect. Yet there are ways of curing even what I regard as the very worst type of congenital criminal at the present day."

"I wish I knew of some!" said Mr. Vinson cheerily. "But what, may I ask, do you regard as the very worst type of congenital criminal at the present day?"

"The society type," replied the crime doctor without an instant's hesitation.

His host permitted himself to open his eyes once more.

"Your ideas are rather sensational, aren't they, Doctor Dollar?"

"It's rather a sensational age, isn't it, Mr. Vinson? Your twentieth-century criminal, with his telephone and his motor-car—for professional purposes—his high explosives and his scientific tools, has got to be an educated person, to begin with; and I am afraid there's an increasing number of educated people who have got to be criminals or else paupers all their lives. A vicious circle, I think you must agree?"

"If you can square it with the truth."

"Isn't it almost a truism, Mr. Vinson? When society women making a living out of bridge, traffic in tickets for Royal enclosures, charge a fat fee for a presentation at Court, and a small fortune for launching an unlikely family in their own set, there must be some reason for it apart from their own depravity. They are no more naturally depraved than I am, but their purse is perhaps even smaller, and their wants are certainly ten times as great. Cupidity is not the motive power; it's simple shortage of the needful—from their point of view. Society increases and multiplies in everything but money, and transmits its expensive tastes without the means to indulge them. So we get our good ladies with their tariff of introductions, and our members of the best clubs always ready for a deal over a horse or a car or anything else that's going to bring them in a fiver. It's a short step from that sort of thing to a shady trick, and from a shady trick to

14

downright crime. But it's a step often taken by the type I mean—though not necessarily with their eyes open. And that's just where the crime doctor should come in."

"In opening their eyes?"

"In saving 'em from themselves while they're still worth saving; in that prevention which is not only better than cure, but the vital principle of modern therapeutics in every other direction. In keeping good material out of prison at all costs, Mr. Vinson, and even though you turn your prisons into country houses with feather beds and moral entertainments every night in life!"

The Secretary of State smiled again, but this time with some sympathy and much less restraint. He was beginning to see some method in what had seemed at first unmitigated mania, and to take some interest in a point of view at least novel and entertaining. But the prison system was not to be attacked, even in terms of fantastic levity, without protest from its official champion.

"Prisons, my dear Doctor Dollar, exist for the benefit of those who keep out of them rather than those who will insist on getting in. Of course, the ideal thing would be to benefit both sides; and that's what we're aiming at all the time. It isn't our fault if a man who gets into quod is a marked man ever after; he shouldn't get into quod."

"You've put your finger on your own vulnerable point!" cried the eager doctor. "Why should he be a marked man?

Why force a professional status on the mere dabbler in crime, who might never have dabbled again? It isn't as if it undid anything he's done; even hanging your murderer doesn't bring your victim back to life, and the chances are that he would never want to murder anybody else. On the other hand, how many serious crimes might be hushed up without anybody being a bit worse off than they were the very moment after their commission!"

Mr. Vinson had been framing an ironical rebuke in the name of morality and the Mosaic law; but he was not sorry to drop the irony and pin his opponent down.

"I hope, Doctor Dollar, it is not to be a function of the new faculty to collaborate in the concealment of crime and criminals?"

"It is impossible," replied the enthusiast, duly drawn, "to define the scope of an embryonic science. When the crime doctor has come to stay—as he will—I can see him playing a Protean part with the full sanction of his profession and of the law. He will be preventive officer, private detective, and father confessor in one, if not even privileged accessory after some awful fact. The humbler pioneer can hope for no such powers; his only chance is to work in the dark on his own lines, to use his own judgment and to take his own risks as I've done to-night. If he really can save a man by screening him, let him do it and blow the odds! If he can stop a thing without giving it away, all the better for everybody, and if he fails to stop it all the worse for him! Let him be a law unto his patient and himself, but let him stand the racket if his law won't work."

"In other words, you would tackle character as ordinary doctors and persons devote themselves to the body and the soul?"

"It would come to that, Mr. Vinson. It's a large order, I know, and I don't expect to see the goods delivered in my time. It will take better men than I am, and many of 'em, even to start delivery on the scale I dream about. But that's the idea all right. Punishment has never signified prevention; what we want is to get under the criminal's skin *before* we make it smart, if not before there's an actual criminal in the case at all!"

"A very plausible confession of faith, Doctor Dollar."

The Minister's tone was dry after the other, but that was all. His fixed eyes seemed to be looking through the doctor's into the scheme itself, probing it on its merits in the very spirit in which it had been propounded. It is only the small men who laugh in the face of genuine enthusiasm, however wild and flighty it may seem. Topham Vinson was not a small man; but he, too, had been guilty of some wild flights in his day, and office had not altogether clipped his wings. The sportsman and the charlatan within him were only too ready to see themselves in another, to hear their own voices on other lips. But the appeal to temperament does not necessarily compromise the mind. And that citadel still flew a neutral flag.

"What about the practise?" asked Topham Vinson, forcing himself back to facts.

"Rome took less building than a London practise, by an unknown man striking out a new line for himself."

"I really don't wonder. Who would come to consult you about a homicidal tendency, or a trick of tampering with special offertories?"

"In the first instance, most likely, the patient's people; then they might send him to see me on some other pretext."

"And what form would the treatment take?"

"It would depend, of course, upon the case. They don't all know that they're being treated for incipient criminality. The majority think they are in an ordinary nursing home."

"A home!" cried the Secretary of State. The word had brought him to his feet at last, in a frame of mind no longer to be concealed by nods and smiles. "You don't mean to tell me, Doctor Dollar, that you actually run a nursing home for unconvicted criminals?"

"Potential criminals, Mr. Vinson. I have at present no patient who is actually wanted by the police."

"And where is this extraordinary establishment?"

"Under my own roof here in Welbeck Street."

"A few hundred yards from where we stand, yet this is the first I hear of it!"

"I can see that. It's not my fault, sir. I have done my best to bring it before your notice."

"How?"

"By writing many times to tell you all about myself and the home, Mr. Vinson."

"Then I never saw the letters. A Home Secretary stands to be shot at by every crank who can hold a pen. I employ more than one young gentleman expressly to divert that sort of fire. You should have got an introduction to me, Doctor Dollar."

The doctor had smiled at an expression that he could not but take to himself. His smile sweetened under the kindlier tone which succeeded that one unmeasured word.

"I am not sorry I waited for the introduction which time has given me, Mr. Vinson."

"You wanted me to assist the good work, I take it?"

"By your countenance and influence—if you could."

"I must see something of it first. I must inspect this home of yours, Doctor Dollar."

The steel eyes of the Vinsons could seldom have cut deeper at a glance, or been met by a pair more candid and unafraid. And yet there was just that cruel suspicion of a cast, to prejudice both the candor and the courage of the finer face.

"It is open to your inspection day or night," said Doctor Dollar.

"Even at this hour? Even to-night?"

The Home Secretary sounded as keen as he looked; but on the other side there was now just enough hesitation to correspond with that one slight flaw in the finer eyes.

"This minute, by all means," said the doctor, with resolute cordiality. "There's always somebody up, and the patients can be seen without being disturbed."

"Then," said the Home Secretary, "it's a chance at a time when every moment of the day is full. Let us strike, doctor, while the iron is as hot as I can assure you that you have made it."

II

That deplorable passion for adventure, which had turned the hope of the last Opposition into a guerrilla warrior in South Africa, but which the Home Secretary of England might have subdued before accepting his portfolio, was by no means a dead volcano as Topham Vinson sallied forth with his extraordinary companion. It was to be noticed that he took with him a thick stick instead of an umbrella, though the deserted streets had become moist with a midnight drizzle. What he expected can only be surmised.

But the odds are that it did not include the shriek of a police-whistle in the sedate region of Wigmore Street, and the instantaneous bolting of Doctor Dollar round the first corner to the left!

Now, the Secretary of State was one of those men who keep up their games out of a cold-blooded regard for the figure; he considered himself as fit at forty as any man in England, and he gave chase with his usual confidence. But the long-legged doctor would have left him behind with the lamp-posts, but for the fact that he was really tearing toward the sound, not flying from it as his pursuer was so ready to suppose. In a matter of seconds they had both fetched up at a brilliantly lighted house, where a more than usually obese policeman was alternately pounding on the door and splitting the sober welkin with his whistle.

"Stop that infernal row!" cried Doctor Dollar, with incensed authority. "Out of the way with you—this is my house!"

And the Home Secretary arrived on the scene of an imminent assault on his police, just in time to divert the outraged officer's attention by asking what had happened, while the doctor found his key.

"Lord only knows!" said the policeman, kicking some broken glass on one side. "Murder, it sounds like; there's somebody been loosing off——"

And even as he spoke somebody loosed off again! The terrific report was followed by screams within and a fresh shower of glass from the fanlight. But by this time Doctor Dollar had his latch-key in the lock. If the door had opened outward, a tangled trio would have fallen into the street; as it was, it hardly would open for the man in white who was struggling with a woman (in red flannel) and a boy (in next to nothing) on the mat.

Dollar exclaimed "Barton!" in blank amazement. But it was not the unlucky Barton who had run amuck. "They won't let me at him! They'll get the lot of us shot dead!" he spluttered, with ungrateful objurgations; and then the newcomers grasped the situation. On the stairs, at the end of the narrow passage, they beheld an enormous revolver, against a background of pink sleeping-suit, with a ferocious eye looking down the barrel.

The crime doctor slipped in front of the Hogarthian group, and stood between everybody and the armed man— shaking his head with an expression that nobody else could see.

"Ozzie, I'm surprised at you!" they heard him say with severity. "I thought you were a better sportsman than to go playing the fool the one night I'm out. If you want to frighten people, do it where you don't damage their property; if you mean murder, I'm your mark, my lad! Aim at my waistcoat buttons and perhaps you'll get me in the mouth; that's better; now blaze away!"

But the pink-striped miscreant was not lowering his barrel to improve his aim. He lowered it altogether. And his other wild eye was open now, and both were blinking with unlovely woe.

"I—I didn't mean any harm," he faltered. "It was only a rag—and I'll pay for the door."

"It'll be a great rag, won't it, if you fire bang into your own foot? Better give me that thing before you do." Dollar held out the steadiest of hands. "No, t'other way round if you don't mind; 'tisn't manners to pass knives and forks business-end first. Ta! Now make yourself scarce before Barton goes for you by kind permission of his family."

The young man in pink stood wildly staring, then fled up-stairs with a smothered sob.

"After him, Barton, before he does something silly," said the doctor under his breath. "My dear Mrs. Barton, you shall tell me the whole thing from A to Z in the morning; go down to bed like a good soul, and be satisfied that you prevented bloodshed. Bobby, take one of the decanters from the tantalus and give your mother a good nightcap." He turned round as the unpresentable pair made off. The street-door was shut; the Home Secretary had sole possession of the mat. "Why, Mr. Vinson, what's happened to the myrmidon?"

"I thought you would like me to get rid of him," said Topham Vinson dryly. "He's waiting outside to explain matters to the reinforcements—as a joke."

"Rather an unconvincing joke!" said the doctor, wiping his forehead with the back of his hand.

"I'm glad you admit it, Doctor Dollar. Am I to understand that the whole thing was a practical joke, carefully rehearsed for my benefit?"

The doctor opened his shining eyes.

"Does it look like one? Hark back a little, Mr. Vinson!"

"There's no need. I didn't think of it till you put the word into my mouth. But it's well, rather a coincidence, doctor, coming on top of the one about my watch—and you of all men catching the thief!"

"Yet this is the sort of thing that's always liable to happen when one's back is turned, and always will be until——"

"Yes?" said the Home Secretary, as Dollar paused and looked at him.

"Until you make it at least as difficult to buy revolvers and ammunition, Mr. Vinson, as a dose of prussic acid! Here's a young man, unsteady, and an epileptic, who has just been placed under my care. I don't run a private asylum, nor is he ripe for one. I must give him his head a little, and this happens in a minute! If it should lead to fresh revolver regulations—but I mustn't forget myself in my excitement.

If you would come in here and smoke a cigarette, I shall have to make a round directly to see how things are quieting down, and should be only too glad to take you with me."

The round was made after further conversation in a dining-room as Spartan as the rest of the crime doctor's characteristic abode. An instructed taste in aged but uncomfortable oak gave it the chill severity of a refectory; and the suggestion was strengthened by a glance into the minute consulting-room next door, which struck the visitor, perhaps in the light of one of Dollar's own similitudes, as a sort of monkish cell and confessional in one. The carven table, rugged yet elaborate, pale with age, might once have been an altar; the chair behind it was certainly an ecclesiastical chair. The cumbrous pieces were yet the fruit of a fastidious eye, and apparently its only fruit. Everything else throughout the house was ultra-sanitary, refreshingly utilitarian, twentieth century. No shred nor thread made for dust on the linoleum, no picture harbored it on the glazed paper. Walls and floors were of the same uncompromising type up-stairs and down. Yet, when a peep was taken through one of the numbered doors above, hothouse flowers bloomed in glass bowls on glass tables, and the bedroom ware was glass again. The very books were bound in glassy vellum; there was a pile of them beside the bed, in which a very young man, swathed in bandages, lay reading under the green glass shade of an electric lamp.

The doctor expressed his sorrow for the occurrence down-stairs; the patient, scarcely looking up, said that since he could not have moved to save his life, he had gone on reading all the time; and they left him at it, obviously glad to be rid of them.

"That," whispered the doctor on the landing, "is a young fellow who will one day be—well, never mind! Until he came to me he had never of his own free will read anything but a bad novel or a newspaper; he is now deep in the immortal work of another weak young man who was swayed by strength, and is himself for the time being under Doctor Johnson's salutary thumb."

"What was his weakness?"

"Pyromania."

"*What?*"

"A passion for setting places on fire. He started it as quite a small boy; they licked it out of him then. All his boyhood he went in fear of the rod, and it kept him straight. Only the other day he goes up to Oxford, and promptly sets fire to his rooms."

"Some form of atavism, I presume?"

"A very subtle case, if I were free to give you its whole history."

"I should be even more interested in your treatment."

"Well, I needn't tell you that he's bandaged up for burns; but you might not guess that he has come by this lot since I've had him, if not almost at my hands."

"Nonsense, man!"

"At any rate I'm responsible for what happened, and it's going to cure him. It was a case of undisciplined imagination acting on a bonnet with just one bee in it. He had never realized what a hell let loose a fire really was; now he *knows* through his own skin."

The statesman's eyebrows were like the backs of two mutually displeased cats.

"But surely that's an old wives' trick pushed beyond all bounds?"

"Pushed further than I intended, Mr. Vinson, I must confess. I only meant him to see a serious fire. So I arranged with the brigade to ring me up when there was a really bad one, and with my man to take the boy out at night for all his walks. There was another good reason for that; and altogether nothing can have seemed more natural than the way they both appeared on the scene of this ghastly riding-school affair."

"I know what's coming!" cried the Home Secretary. "This is the fellow who dashed in to help save the horses, and got away afterward without giving his name!"

"That's it. He says he'll hear those horses till his dying hour! He was in the thick of it before Barton or anybody else could stop him—they only succeeded in stopping poor Barton from following. Well, I can take no credit for the very last thing I should have dreamt of allowing; but I fancy the odds are fairly long that the tempting element will never, never again tempt our young friend up-stairs!"

They had drifted down again during this recital; and he who had led the way stood staring at the crime doctor, in his monkish cell, with that intent inscrutability which was one of Topham Vinson's most effective masks; but now it was a mask imperfectly adjusted, with the warm light of admiration breaking through, and the shadow of something else interfering with that light. When Doctor Dollar had marched upon the loaded revolver, talking down the barrel as to an infant pointing a popgun—daring another daredevil to shoot him dead—the same admiring look had come over the face behind him, qualified in precisely the same fashion. But then the doctor had not seen it, and now it made him wince a little, as though he dreaded something that was bound to come.

This was what came:

"Doctor Dollar, I should prefer not to ask you to show me or tell me any more. I know a good man when I see one, and I know good work when I catch him at it. Perhaps that was necessary in the case of such extraordinary work as yours; yet you say it was a sheer coincidence that I caught you at it to-night—or rather that such tough work was waiting for you when we got here?"

"Do you still doubt it? Why, you yourself insisted on coming round to see the place in the middle of this blessed night!"

"Exactly. That establishes your second coincidence; but with all respect, doctor, I don't believe in two of the same sort on the same night to the same two people!"

"What was the other coincidence?" demanded the doctor, huskily.

"Your catching *any* old pickpocket with my watch—and letting him off! Come, doctor, do one more thing for me, and I'll do all in my power for you and your great work. That is, of course, if you still want me to take the interest I certainly should have taken if I had seen your letters."

"If!" cried the young man from the fulness of his heart. "Your interest is the one thing I do want of you, and you are the one person I want to interest!"

His eyes shone like big brown lamps, straight enough now in their intensity, and dim with the glory of their vision. He could tremble, too, it seemed, where the stake was not dear life, but a life's dearer work. And Topham Vinson was almost moved himself; he really was absorbed and thrilled; but not to the detriment of his penetrative astuteness, his political instinct for a bargain.

"Come, then," said he: "show me the fellow who sneaked my watch."

"Show him to you? What do you mean?"

The doctor had not started. But the injured eye showed its injury once more.

"It was one of your patients who picked my pocket," said the Home Secretary, with as much confidence as though he had known it all the time. "Would you have been in such a hurry to wash your hands of anybody else, and to undo what he'd done?"

Dollar made no answer, no denial; but he glanced at a venerable one-handed clock, whose unprotected pendulum shaved the wall with noisy sweeps. It was two o'clock in the morning, but already night must have been turned into dreadful and disturbing day for all the inmates. The doctor abandoned that excuse unmade, and faced his visitor in desperation.

"So you want to see him—now?"

"I do. I have my reasons. But it shall end at that—if I do see him. *That* won't nip my goodwill in the bud!" It was obvious what would.

"You shall see him," said the doctor, as though racking his mind once more. "But there are difficulties you perhaps can't quite appreciate. It means giving away a patient—don't you see?"

"Perfectly. It seems to me a very proper punishment, since it's all he'll get. Yet you don't want to lose your hold. Couldn't you send him down here on some pretext, instead of taking me up to him?"

The crime doctor's face lit up as if by electricity.

"I can and I will!" he cried. "Wait here, Mr. Vinson. He's another reader; he shall come down for a book!"

The great man waited with the satisfaction of a slightly overbearing personality for once very nearly overborne. He was now intensely interested in the crime doctor and his unique establishment. It was an interest that he had no intention of sharing with his closest colleague, until he had gone deeper into a theory and practise that were already a revelation to him. They might both prove unworkable on any large scale, and yet they might light the way to sensational legislation of the very type that Topham Vinson was the very man to introduce. Boundless ambition was one of the forces of a nature that responded to the call of any sufficiently dazzling crusade; but the passion for adventure ran ambition hard; and a crusade calculated to gratify both appetites was dazzling even to eyes of triple steel!

Only, he must show this new ally his power before they struck up their alliance; that was the great reason for insisting on seeing the pickpocket. But there was a little reason besides. An excellent memory had supplied Mr. Vinson with a kind of post-impression of the pickpocket.

And within one minute of the doctor's departure, and one second of the patient's prompt appearance, a certain small suspicion had been confirmed.

"I think we've met before, my man?" he had begun. His man started stagily—was altogether of the stage—a bearded scarecrow in rags too ragged to be true. Vinson found the switches and made more light. "Not half a bad disguise," he continued, "whoever you may be! I suppose they're supplied on the premises for distinguished patients?"

"How do you know it's a disguise?" croaked the hairy man, with downcast eyes.

"Well, you don't look a distinguished patient, do you?" said the Home Secretary airily. "On the other hand, your kit doesn't convince me at all; looks to me as if it would fall to pieces but for what the ladies call a foundation—eh?"

And he swooped down on the ragged tails as their owner turned a humiliated back. And the "foundation" was a perfectly good overcoat turned inside out; moreover, it was a coat that Topham Vinson seemed to know; it was a coat that he suddenly remembered, as he shot up to his full height and then stood deadly still.

The pickpocket had not turned round. But his wig and beard lay at his elbow on the mantelpiece; his diminished head had sunk into his hands; and the electric light blazed upon a medallion of silver hair, up above one burning ear.

"Doctor—Dollar!" exclaimed Topham Vinson. And the ingenuous ring of his own startled voice only added to his sense of outrage.

"Yes! I was the man.... It was only to get at you—you know that!"

It was a hoarse voice muttering to the wall, in a dire discomfiture that had its effect on the insulted Minister.

"So that was your weakness!" The plain comment was icier than any sneer. "Picking and stealing—and your hand still keeps its cunning!"

"Yes. That was how my wound had taken me." There was less shame in the hoarse voice, thanks to the bracing coldness of the other. "It started in the field hospital—orderlies laughed and encouraged me—nurses at Netley just as bad! Everybody treated it as a joke; the doctor used to ask for his watch or his handkerchief after every visit; and the great score was when he thought I had one, and it was really the other—or both—or the keys out of his trousers pocket! It amused the ward and made me popular—made me almost suicidal—because I alone knew that I couldn't help doing it to save my life.... And the rest *you* know."

"I do, indeed!"

"This beastly kit, I had it made on purpose so that I could run after you one minute with what I'd taken from you the minute before! It was a last attempt to gain your ear—to get you interested. And now——"

"And now," said Topham Vinson, with a kind hand on the bent shoulders, yet a keen eye on the bent head—"and now I suppose you think you've put the lid on it? So you have, my dear doctor—on any sneaking doubts I had about you! You've struck a job after my own heart, and you've led me into it as I never was led into anything in my life before. Well, you've just got to keep me in it now; and I'm conceited enough to believe I shall be worth my place. Don't you think you might turn round, Doctor Dollar, and let us shake hands on that?"

II

THE LIFE-PRESERVER

The Lady Vera Moyle had made herself notorious in a cause that scored some points through her allegiance. She it was who cajoled the Home Secretary outside Palace Yard, and sent him about his weighty business with the colors of a hated Union pinned to his unconscious back. It is true that some of her excesses had less to redeem them, but all were committed with a pious zest which recalled the saying that the Moyles were a race of Irish rebels who had intermarried with the saints. It was reserved for Lady Vera to combine the truculence of her forefathers with the serene solemnity of their wives, and to enact her devilments, as she took their consequences, with a buxom austerity all her own.

But she was not at her best when she went to see Doctor Dollar on Christmas Eve; for it was just two months after the autumn raid, which had caused the retirement of Lady Vera Moyle, and some of her political friends, for precisely that period. Otherwise, the autumn raid had been a triumph for the raiders, thanks to a fog of providential density, which had fought on their side as the stars in their courses fought against Sisera for the earliest militant. Never had private property been destroyed on so generous a scale, with fewer casualties on the side of the destroying angels; and yet there had been one unnecessary blot on the proceedings, which they were the first to repudiate and condemn.

A vile male member of the common criminal classes had not only taken occasion to loot a jeweler's window, broken by some innocent lady, but had coolly murdered a policeman who interfered with him in the perpetration of his selfish crime. Fortunately the wretch had been traced through the stolen trinkets, expeditiously committed and condemned, and was on the point of paying the supreme penalty. No sane person could doubt his guilt, and yet there were those who sought to fix a certain responsibility on the women! The charge of moral complicity had disgraced and stultified both Press and platform, and the Home Secretary, pestered for a reprieve, had only sealed the murderer's fate at the eleventh hour. Even the steel nerves of the Vinsons had suffered under a complex strain: it was just as well that he was on the point of departure for the holidays.

A deplorable circumstance was the way the Minister's last hours in town had been embittered by his implacable tormentor, Lady Vera Moyle. That ingrate had celebrated her release by trying to invade the Home Office, and by actually waylaying the Secretary of State in Whitehall. An unobtrusive body-guard had nipped the annoyance in the bud; but it had caused Topham Vinson to require champagne at his club, whither he was proceeding on the arm of his last ally and most secret adviser, Doctor John Dollar of Welbeck Street. And before dark the doctor had been invaded in his turn.

"You must blame the Home Secretary for this intrusion," began Lady Vera, with all the precision of a practised speaker who knew what she had to say. "He refused, as you heard, to listen to what I had to say to him this morning; but the detective-in-waiting informed me that you were not only a friend of Mr. Vinson's, but yourself a medical expert in criminology. I have therefore a double reason for coming to you, Doctor Dollar, though it would not have been necessary if Mr. Topham Vinson had treated me with ordinary courtesy."

"I am very glad you have done so, Lady Vera," rejoined the doctor in his most conciliatory manner. "Mr. Vinson, to be frank with you, is not in a fit state for the kind of scene he was afraid you were going to make. He is in a highly nervous condition for a man of his robust temperament. Truth, Lady Vera, compels me to add that you and your friends have had something to do with this, but the immediate cause is a far more unhappy case which he has just settled."

"*Has* he settled it?" cried Lady Vera, turning paler than before between her winter sables and a less seasonable hat.

"This morning," said Dollar, with a very solemn air.

"He isn't going to hang that poor man?"

No breath came between the opened lips that prison had bleached and parched, but neither did they tremble as the doctor bowed.

"If you mean Alfred Croucher," said he, "convicted of the murder of Sergeant Simpkins during the last suffragist disturbance, I can only say there would be an end of capital punishment if he had been reprieved."

"Doctor Dollar," returned Lady Vera, under great control, "it was about this case, and nothing else, that I wanted to speak to the Home Secretary. I never heard of it until this morning, for I have been out of the way of newspapers, as you may know; and it is difficult to take in a whole trial at one hurried reading. Do you mind telling me why everybody is so sure that this man is the murderer? Did anybody see him do it?"

The crime doctor smiled as he shook his head.

"Very few murders are actually witnessed, Lady Vera; yet this would have been one of the few, but for the fog. Croucher was plainly seen through the jeweler's window, helping himself one moment, then struggling with the unfortunate sergeant."

"Was the struggle seen as plainly as the robbery?"

"Not quite, perhaps, but the evidence was equally convincing about both. Then the stolen goods were found, some of them, still in Croucher's possession; and the way he tried to account for that, in the witness-box, was only less suicidal than his fatal attempt at an alibi."

"Poor fool!" exclaimed Lady Vera, with perhaps less pity than impatience. "Of course he was there—I saw him!"

Dollar was not altogether unprepared for this.

"You were there yourself, then, Lady Vera?"

"I should think I was!"

"It—it wasn't you who broke the window for him?"

"Of course it was! Yet nobody tried to find me as a witness! It is only by pure chance that I come out in time to save an innocent man's life, for innocent he is of everything but theft. *I* know—too well!"

Her voice was no longer under inhuman control; and there was something in its passionate pitch that sent a cold thrill of conviction down Dollar's spine. He gazed in horror at the unhappy girl, in her luxurious sables, drawn up to her last inch in the pitiless glare of his electric light; and even as he gazed—and guessed—all horror melted into the most profound emotion he had ever felt. It was she who first found her voice, and now it was calmer than it had been as yet.

"One thing more about the trial," she said. "What was the weapon he is supposed to have used?"

"His knife."

"Yet it seems to have been a small wound?"

"It had a small blade."

"But was there any blood on it?"

She had to press him for these details; any squeamishness was on his side, and he a doctor!

"There was," he said. "Croucher had an explanation, but it wasn't convincing."

"The truth often isn't," said Lady Vera, bitterly. "You may be surprised to hear that the blow wasn't struck with a knife at all. It was struck with—this!"

Her right hand flew from her glossy muff; in it was no flashing steel, but a short, black, round-knobbed life-preserver, that she handed over without more words.

"But his skull wasn't smashed!" exclaimed John Dollar, and for an instant he looked at his visitor with the eye of the alienist. "It was a puncture of the carotid artery, and you couldn't do that with this if you tried."

"Hit the floor with it," said Lady Vera, "but don't hold it quite by the end."

Dollar bent down and did as directed; at the blow, a poniard flew out of the opposite end to the round knob; the point caught in his sleeve.

"That's how it was done," continued Lady Vera. "And I am the person it was done by, Doctor Dollar!"

"It was—an accident?" he said, hoarsely. He could look at her as though the accident had not been fatal; he had less command of his voice.

"I call it one; the law may not," said she resignedly. "Yet I didn't even know that I possessed such a weapon as this; it was sold to me as a life-preserver, and nothing else, out of a pawnbroker's window, where I happened to see it on the very morning of the raid. I thought it would be just the thing for smashing other windows, especially with that thong to go round one's wrist. I thought, too—I don't mind telling you—that, if I were roughly handled, it was a thing I could use in self-defense as I couldn't very well use a hammer."

And here she showed no more shame than a soldier need feel about his bayonet after battle; and Dollar met her eyes on better terms. He had been making mechanical experiments with the life-preserver. Some spring was broken. That was why it became a dagger at every blow, instead of only when you gave it a jerk.

"And you were roughly handled by Sergeant Simpkins?" he suggested eagerly.

"Very," she said, with a certain reluctance. "But I expect the poor fellow was as excited as I was when I tried to beat him off."

"I suppose you hardly knew what you were doing, Lady Vera?"

"Not only that, Doctor Dollar, but I didn't know what I had done."

"Thank God for that!"

"But did you imagine it for a moment? That's the whole point and explanation of everything that has happened. The worst was over in a few seconds, in the thick of that awful fog, but, of course I never dreamt what I had done. I did think that I had knocked him out. But that was all that ever entered my head until this very morning."

"Were you close to your broken window at the time?"

"Very close, and yet out of sight in the fog."

"And you had seen nothing of this man Croucher, and his hand in the affair?"

"Not after I'd done my part. I did just before. I'm certain it was the same huge man that they describe. But I heard the whole thing while we were struggling. They were blowing a police-whistle and calling out 'Thieves!' I remember hoping that the policeman would hear them, and let me go. But I suppose his blood was up, as well as mine."

"And after you had—freed yourself?" said the doctor, trying not to set his teeth.

"I ran off, of course! I knew that I had done much more than I ever intended; but that's all I knew, or suspected, even when I found this horrid thing open in my hand. I tried to shut it again, but couldn't. So I hid it in my dress, and ran up Dover Street to my club, where I put it straight into a bag that I had there. Then I made myself decent and—turned out again with a proper hammer."

The doctor groaned; he could not help it. Yet it was his first audible expression of disapproval; he had restrained himself while all the worst was being told; and the girl's face acknowledged his consideration. Her color had come at last. Thus far, in recounting her intentional misdeeds, as though they were all in the great day's work, she had shown a divine indifference to his opinion of her or her proceedings. There had been nothing aggressive about it—he merely doubted whether the question of his views had ever entered her mind. But now he could see that it did; he had shown her something that she did not want to lose, and her fine candor hid that fact as little as any other.

"I didn't know what I'd done, remember!" she said with sharp solicitude. "I never did know until this morning, when I heard of the case for the first time, and for the first time saw the stains on the dagger—at which you've been trying so hard not to look! Do look at them, Doctor Dollar. Of course, there can be no doubt what they are, but I shall be only too glad for you to prove it to everybody's satisfaction."

"'Only too glad,' Lady Vera?"

They gazed at each other for several seconds. Her face was tragic to him now; but emotion, apparently, was the one thing she would condescend to hide. But for her eyes, she might have been incredibly callous and cold-blooded; her blue Irish eyes were great and glassy with a grief not soluble in tears.

43

"Doctor Dollar," she said, tensely, "nothing can undo this hideous thing, though I hope to live long enough to make such poor amends as a human being can. But in this other direction they must be made at once. It's no use thinking of what can't be undone till we *have* undone what we can—if we are quick! That's why I tried to go straight to the Home Secretary, and why I have come straight to you. Take me to him, Doctor Dollar, and help me to convince him that what I have told you is the whole truth and nothing else! If you think it will make it easier, satisfy yourself about those blood-stains. Then we can take the dagger with us."

The doctor applied a crude test on the spot. He stooped over the fire, heated the stained steel between the bars, cooled it at the open window, picked off a scale and examined it briefly under a microscope. All this was done with tremendous energy tempered by extreme precision and nicety. And Lady Vera followed the operation with an impersonal interest that could not but include the operator, so intent upon his task, so obviously thankful to have a task of any sort in hand. But when he rose from his microscope it was with a shrug of the shoulders, an almost angry shake of the head.

"Of course, this is all no good, you know!" he cried, as if it were her test. "It would take hours to make the analysis that's really wanted."

"But as far as you have gone, Doctor Dollar?"

"As far as I have gone—which isn't a legal or medical inch—it certainly does look like blood, Lady Vera."

"Of course it is blood. There's another thing that will help us, too."

"What's that?"

"One of the best points in the defense, so far as I've had time to make out, was about the prisoner's knife. Now, if we take this with us, either to the Home Secretary, or, if he still refuses to see me, to New Scotland Yard——"

"Lady Vera!" the doctor interrupted, aghast at her suicidal zeal. "Is it possible that you realize the position you are in? It isn't only a situation that you've got to face; that you have already done, superbly! But have you any conception of the consequences?"

"I think I have," said Lady Vera, smiling. "I don't believe they will hang me; it would be affectation to pretend I did. But, of course, that's their business—mine is to change places with an innocent man."

"That you will never do," replied the doctor warmly. "There's no innocent man in the case; this Croucher is a thief and a perjurer, besides being an old convict who has spent half his life in prison! He would have had five years for the other night's work, without any question of a murder; they'll simply pack him off to Dartmoor or Portland when we've saved his miserable neck. And save it we will, no fear about that; but at what a price—at what a price!"

45

"I don't see that you need trouble about it," said Lady Vera, concerned at his distress, "beyond putting me in touch with Mr. Vinson. The rest will be up to him, as they say; and, after all, it won't be anything so very terrible to me. I am an old prisoner myself, you must remember!"

There was a gleam of her notorious audacity with all this; but it was like the glow of flowers on a grave. The horror of things to happen had never possessed her valiant eyes, and yet it must have been there, for all at once Dollar missed it. He read her look. He had relieved her mind about the man in the cell, only to open it at last to the man in his grave. Grief crippled her as horror had not; prisons could be broken, but not the prison to which her hand had sent a fellow creature. Yet her grief was mastered in its turn, forced out of sight before his eyes, even while her flippant speech rang through him as the bravest utterance he had ever heard.

It blew a bugle in the man's brain, and the call was clear and definite. He knew his own mind only less instantaneously than he had penetrated hers. Never in all his days had he known his mind quite so well as when she thought better of the very words which had enlightened him, and went on to add to them in another key:

"So now, Doctor Dollar, will you crown all your great kindness by taking me to see the Home Secretary at once?"

"Lady Vera," he exclaimed, with unreasonable irritation, "what is the good of asking impossibilities? I couldn't take you to Topham Vinson even if I would. He would begin by doubting your sanity; there would be all manner of silly difficulties. Moreover, he's not in town."

She showed displeasure at the statement of fact only.

"Doctor Dollar, are you serious?"

"Perfectly."

"Have you forgot that I saw you together at almost two o'clock?"

"I think not quite so late as that. The Home Secretary left Euston at 2:45."

"Where for?"

She looked panic-stricken.

"I'll tell you, Lady Vera, if you promise not to follow him by the next train."

"When does it go?"

"Not for some time. There's only one more; we debated which he should take. But you mustn't take the other, Lady Vera; you must leave that to me. I want you to leave the whole thing to me—from this very moment till you hear from me again."

"When would that be, Doctor Dollar?"

"As soon as I have seen Mr. Vinson."

"You would undertake to tell him everything?"

"Every detail, exactly as you have told me."

"Will it seem credible at second-hand?"

"Quite enough so to justify a respite. That's the first object; and this is the first step to it, believe me! There's plenty of time between this and—Tuesday."

"Oh! I know that," she returned, bluntly disdainful of a well-meant hesitation. "There's still not a moment to lose while that poor man lies facing death."

"I'm not sure that he does, Lady Vera. The decision's only just been made; it won't be out till the day after to-morrow. I don't believe they would break it to Croucher on Christmas Day."

"They can break the good news instead. Where is Mr. Vinson? It's all right, I won't attempt to tackle him till you have. That's a promise—and I don't break them like windows!"

John Dollar ignored that boast with difficulty. He saw through her tragic levity as through a glass, and his heart cried out with a sympathy hard indeed to keep to himself; but it was obviously the last thing required of him by Lady Vera Moyle. He gave her the required information in a voice only less well managed than her own. And he thought her eyes softened with the faintest recognition of his restraint.

"I thought the Duke had washed his hands of his notorious nephew," she remarked. "Well, we shall have to spoil the family gathering, I'm afraid."

"That's my job, Lady Vera."

"And I never thanked you for taking it on! Nor will I, Doctor Dollar; thanks don't meet a case like this!" Very frankly she took his hand instead: it was hotter and less steady than her own. "And now what about your train?"

"I'm afraid there's not one till seven o'clock. Vinson talked of going down by it at first."

The time-table confirmed his fear; he threw it down, and plunged into the telephone directory instead. Lady Vera watched him narrowly. He had dropped into his old oak chair, and the sheen of age on the table betrayed his face as though it were bent over clear brown water. She could see its anxiety as he had not allowed her to see it yet.

"I suppose you wouldn't care to face it in a motor?"

She was faltering for the first time.

"That's exactly what I mean to do," he answered, without looking up from the directory. "I'm just going to telephone for a car."

"Then you needn't!" she cried joyfully. "We have at least two eating their bonnets off in our mews. I'll go home in a taxi, and send one of them straight round with a driver who knows the way, and a coat that you must promise to wear, Doctor Dollar. All my people are away except my mother, and she won't know; she isn't strong enough to use the cars. But I mustn't speak of poor mother, or I shall make a fool of myself yet. It's partly my fault as it is, you see, and of course all this will make her worse. But I'm not so sure of that, either! My mother is the kind of person who has all the modern ailments and no modern ideas—but she could show us all how to play the game at a pinch. She will be the first to back me up in the only conceivable course."

This speech had not come quite so fluently as might be supposed, though Dollar had only interrupted it to send for a taxicab. It had interrupted itself when Lady Vera Moyle was betrayed into speaking of poor Lady Armagh, whose heart-felt disapproval of her daughter's escapades was public property. Dollar had heard from Topham Vinson—that very day at lunch—that the last one had made her seriously ill; then what indeed of impending resolutions, and the nine days' tragic scandal which was the very least that could come of them unless——

"Unless!"

In the doctor's mind so many broken sentences began with that will-o'-the-wisp among words, that others really spoken fell upon stony ears, and he knew as little what he said in reply. In a dream he saw a small hand wave as the taxicab vanished round the corner to the right; in a dream he sprang up-stairs, hiding under his coat the weapon with which that little hand had dealt out death; and awoke in his wintriest clothes, his greatest coat, to find himself called upon to top the lot with another of unkempt fur sent with the car.

That aluminum clipper—a fifteen-horse-power Invincible Talboys—was indeed at the door in incredibly quick time. Twin headlights lit long wedges of London mud; two pairs of goblin goggles mounted up behind them—one sent with the coat and a message that was more than law. The dapper chauffeur huddled down behind the wheel; the passenger sat bolt upright at his side; the Barton family, his faithful creatures, carried out an impromptu tableau in the background. Mother and son—those unpresentable features of a former occasion—now appeared as immaculate cook and page at the top of the area steps and on the lighted threshold respectively. Barton himself leaned out of an upper window, still in his white suit—it was the typically muggy Christmas of a degenerate young century—but with all the black cares of the strange establishment quite apparent on his snowy shoulders. The dapper driver gave his horn a spiteful pinch. And then they were off, only to be held up in Oxford Street by the Christmas traffic, but doing better in the Edgware Road, and soon on the way to Edgware itself, and Elstree and St. Albans, and all the lighted towns and pitch-dark roads that lie by night between the capital of England and her smallest county.

"Least trem-lines this wye," said the dapper one, a mile or two out; and said no more for another fifty. But he drove like a little genius, and the car responded to his cunning hands as a horse that knows its master. She proved to be a sound roadster whose only drawback was a lack of racing speed; the lad had her in prime condition, and the good road ran from under her like silk from a silent loom.

Dollar sat beside him, in the shelter of a wind-screen that glazed and framed a continuous study in nocturnal values. Now the fine shades would be broken by a cluster of lights, soon to scatter and go out like sparks from a pipe; now only by the acetylene lamps that kept the foreground in a blaze between villages. Often a ghostly portent appeared hovering over the road ahead; but this was only the doctor's own anxious face, seen dimly in the screen.

And yet he was not really anxious for those first fifty miles. At the start he was too thankful to be under way, and the road was never empty of exciting and diverting possibilities. But at Bedford they stopped for supper: it was Dollar's sudden idea, the hour being now between eight and nine; but the treasure at the wheel professed his readiness to push on, and it would have been better for Dollar to have taken him at his word. The break in the run also broke up the dreamy lull induced by the keen air and the low smooth hum of the car. In the warm hotel, all holly and Christmas cheer, he came back to real life with a thud, and its most immediate problem beset him all the rest of the way.

Hitherto his one anxiety had been to get at the Home Secretary that night; henceforth he was having the interview over and over again, with a different result every time. He knew, indeed, what he meant to say himself; he had known that before he said good-by to Lady Vera Moyle. But what would the Home Secretary say? Was it conceivable that the blood-stained life-preserver would be enough for him? It would be supported by the sworn statement of a man whom he had learned to trust. But was such utterly indirect evidence in the least likely to upset a decision already taken, if not already communicated to the man in the condemned cell?

The very thought of that hapless wretch was fraught with definite and vivid horror. The crime doctor had once seen the inside of a condemned cell; he could see it still. The door was open, the pitiful occupant at exercise in an adjacent yard. He had looked in. The cell was not so gloomy as it should have been. Texts on the walls, sunlight through the bars, and on the fixed flap of clean worn wood, a big open book.

Dollar recalled every detail with morbid fidelity. He had gone in to look at the book, and found it a bound volume of *Good Words*, open at a laudable serial by a lady then in vogue with the virtuous. Yet that particular reader had cut a woman's throat over a quarrel about a shilling, and Dollar had seen him striding jauntily up and down the narrow yard, cracking some joke with the attendant warders, a smile on his scrubby lips and in his bold blue eyes. He could see the fellow as he had seen him for ten seconds years ago. Yet his pity for one in the same awful case, for a crime he had not committed, was as nothing to his infinite sorrow and compassion for her who had committed it unawares, comparatively light as the punishment for such a deed was bound to be.

But was it? Not for Lady Vera Moyle, at all events! Either she would go scot-free, or her punishment might well be worse than death. It might easily kill her mother; then the tragedy would be a double tragedy after all, and Lady Vera would still be its author. Supposing she had not discovered her own crime! Croucher would have been no loss to the community; life-long criminals like Croucher were best out of the way, murderers or no murderers. The crime doctor was convinced of that. They were the incurables; extermination was the only thing for them.

"I would shut up my penitentiaries, but enlarge my lethal chamber," he sometimes said, and would be quite serious about it. Yet not for a moment could he have carried his ideas to their logical conclusion in the concrete case of Alfred Croucher and Lady Vera Moyle. He could have let a man of that stamp go technically innocent to the gallows— or he thought he could just then. But he could not have allowed the greatest monster to suffer for Lady Vera's sins— and that he felt in his bones. It was the personal equation as supplied by her that made the thing impossible. Such a load on such a soul! Better any punishment than that!

At Kettering a right-hand turn led up-hill and down-dale into little Rutland, and Dollar ceased glaring at his own ghost in the wind-screen; a healthily immediate anxiety kept him peering at his watch instead. But now they were skirting one of the longest and stumpiest stone walls in feudal England, and all of a sudden it parted in twin turrets joined by triple gates. Over the central arch heraldic monsters pawed the stars; underneath an arc lamp hung resplendent; all three gates were open, and the drive beyond was a perspective of guiding lights. It was evidently a case of Christmas festivities on a suitable scale at Stockersham Hall.

Miles up the drive, a semicircle of motor-cars fringed a country edition of the Horseguards Parade, dominated by an escaped hotel; and the car that really was from London had becoming palpitations in the zone of light. Before a comparatively simple portico a superlatively splendid menial looked askance at the doctor's borrowed furs, but was not unimpressed by a curt inquiry for Mr. Topham Vinson, and consented to inquire in his turn.

"Be quick and quiet, and give him this card," said the doctor, slipping half-a-sovereign underneath it. "I want to see Mr. Vinson—no one else—on urgent business from the Home Office."

Yet the next minute merely brought forth an imposing personage whom the dapper driver did not fail to salute; even Dollar was not positive whether it was the Duke or his butler until summoned indoors with the subtle condescension of the supreme servitor. He went as he was, in hirsute coat and goggles, the butler stalking at arm's length, with an air of personal repudiation happily not lost upon the little London lynx in charge of the car.

That artist would have been an endless joy to eyes not turned within. His silent endurance and efficiency, his phlegmatic zest in an adventure which might have a professional interest for him, but obviously did not engage his curiosity, were qualities which even the tormented Dollar had appreciated at intervals on the road. But now he missed a treat. The little Cockney ran his engine till the first flunkey returned and said things through the noise. Then he looked under his bonnet, as a monkey into its offspring's head. But the climax arrived with sandwiches on a lordly tray, when a glass of beer was sent back, and one of champagne brought instead to this choice specimen of a contemporary type. It was scarcely down before the passenger reappeared, accompanied by another swollen figure in motoring disguise, as well as by my Lord Duke, who saw them off himself, and did look less ducal than the butler after all.

The many lights of Stockersham dwindled and disappeared into the night and one long wave of incandescence flowed back as it had come, by finespun hedge and wirework thicket, through dead villages and sleeping towns, like phosphorescent foam before a vessel's bows. And in the torpedo body of the Invincible Talboys, where Dollar now sat behind his companion of the outward trip, and the Home Secretary of England behind a fat cigar, there was a strained silence through two entire counties, but something like an explosion on the confines of the third.

"Do you still refuse to give her name?" demanded Topham Vinson, exactly as though they had been talking all the time. The stump of his second cigar was so short that angry light and angry mouth were one.

"I must," said Dollar, in a muffled voice, and he pointed to the hunched shoulders within a yard of their noses.

"In that case we have no secrets," replied the Home Secretary with a sneer. "But why must you, Dollar? She seems to have made no reservations with you, yet you would make this enormous one with me."

"It's a secret of the consulting-room, Mr. Vinson; those of the confessional are not more sacred, as you know perfectly well."

"And you expect me to eat my decision on the strength of a hearsay anonymous confession?"

"I do—in the first instance," said Dollar decidedly. "An immediate respite would commit you to nothing, but I don't ask even for that on the unsupported strength of what I told you at Stockersham. You know what you've got in your overcoat pocket. Hand it over to your own analyst; have an exhumation, if you like, and see if the weapon doesn't actually fit the wound; if it doesn't, hang your man."

"I'm much obliged for your valuable advice. But it's got to be one thing or the other, once for all; the poor devil has been on tenter-hooks quite long enough."

"And have you forgotten how nearly you decided in his favor, Mr. Vinson, without all this to turn the scale?"

It was perhaps an ominous feature of their mushroom intimacy that the younger man had not yet been invited to drop the formal prefix in addressing his senior by a short decade. But this would not have been the moment even for a familiarity encouraged in happier circumstances. And yet Dollar dared to pat the great man's arm as he spoke; and the gesture was as the button on the foil; it prevented a shrewd thrust from drawing blood, and if anything it improved Topham Vinson's temper.

"It's no good, my dear fellow!" he exclaimed in friendly settlement of the general question. "I must have the lady's name, unless she's determined to defeat her own ends."

"Do you mean to say that it's her name or Croucher's life?"

Topham Vinson had not meant to say any such thing—in so many words—and it was annoying to have them put into his mouth. But he had decided not to be annoyed any more. It did not pay with this fellow Dollar; at least, it had not paid on that occasion; but anybody might be at a disadvantage after a heavy political strain, a lengthy journey, an excellent dinner, and a development as untimely as it was embarrassing. Mr. Vinson relapsed into silence and an attitude unconsciously modeled on that of the gallant little driver. His body sank deep into the rugs, his head as deep between his shoulders. It was almost Hertfordshire before he spoke again.

"Vera Moyle was one of the Oxford Street division," he remarked at last. "I know all about her movements on the night of battle; otherwise I should want to know about them now. If I thought *she* was the woman——"

"What's that?" said Dollar lethargically. "I was almost asleep."

The remarks did not gain weight by repetition, but the broken sentence was finished with some effect: "I'd let her drain the cup."

"I don't wonder," rejoined Dollar, sympathetically.

"Yet you would have me risk my political existence for one of her kidney!"

"I don't follow."

"You would reprieve the apparent murderer, and let the real one continue militant here on earth?"

"I believe she has had her fill of militancy."

"Not she!"

"I'll go bail for her if you like. It was an accident She is heart-broken about it—and you don't know her—I do! I'd back her not to run the risk of such another accident!"

"And what if she rounded on me? However such a thing came out, it would be my ruin, Dollar."

"It wouldn't come out through her!"

A certain fervor crept into the doctor's voice. It was obviously unconscious, and Topham Vinson was far too astute a person to engender consciousness and caution by so much as a rallying syllable. But he did hazard a leading question, subtly introduced as nothing of the sort.

"I'm not trying to get at what I want in a roundabout way," he had the nerve to state. "I've given up trying to pump you, Dollar; but—would it make a *very* great scandal if we had to fix this thing on this particular young lady?"

"I can't answer about scandals," replied the still not unwary doctor. "It would break hearts—probably cause death—make her a double murderer in her own eyes, and God knows what else as a result! And it wouldn't do anybody the least bit of good, because you would still have to give Croucher a suitable term for his authentic offense."

It was three o'clock on Christmas morning when they saw the lights of London from the top of Brockley Hill; a minute later they were on the tram-lines at the foot, and almost immediately in the purlieus of the town.

The trip did not end without a telling taste of Mr. Vinson's very individual quality. In Maida Vale he suddenly announced his intention of having the life-preserver identified in those very small hours by the pawnbroker who had sold it on the morning of the autumn raid. The crime doctor was terrified; for aught he knew the man might be well aware that he had sold it to Lady Vera Moyle. She was notorious enough, in all conscience; his only hope lay in the fact that he himself had not known her by sight before that day. In vain he raised various objections; they were well met by his own previous arguments for the immediate reprieve of Alfred Croucher, and he feared to press them. He knew only the name of the pawnbroker's street, but here Cockney sharpness came in again, and they were pounding on the right shutters by half past three. An up-stairs window flew alight, up went a sash, and out came an angry head.

"My name is Topham Vinson," said one of the swaddled men in a sepulchral voice. "I'm the Home Secretary, but I can't force you to come down and speak to me because of that. I can only make it more or less worth your while."

He was fishing for his sovereign-case as he spoke. In another minute the private door had shut behind him and Doctor Dollar, and an obsequious sack of humanity shuffled before them into a sanctum still redolent of a somewhat highly-seasoned meal.

"I remember 'aving it in the thop," said the unkempt head protruding from the sack. "But I can't thay 'ow it came here—that I can thwear in a court of juthtith, my lord! It'th a narthy, beathly thing, but I thwear it wath here when I took over the bithneth."

"I don't care how or when it came here," said Topham Vinson, counting the sovereigns in the gold case attached to the watch-chain of other memories. "I want to know if you remember selling this life-preserver?"

"Yeth, I do!"

"When?"

"It would be—let me thee—thome time lartht October or November."

"Do you remember who bought it?"

"Yeth—a young lady!"

Dollar breathed again. The man did not know her name; at first he was extremely shaky on the point of personal appearance. But the doctor assisted him by unscrupulously suggesting a number of marked characteristics which Lady Vera Moyle did not happen to possess. The man fell straight into the trap, recalled every imaginary feature, and finally earned big gold by quite convincingly connecting the sale of the life-preserver with the date of the great women's raid. Mr. Vinson looked very stern as he led the way out into the street; and it was he who sharply woke the little chauffeur, who was snoring heartily over his wheel.

"I like that lad," he muttered in the car. "He does nothing by halves. No more do I! Do you mind dropping me first at Portman Square?"

Dollar gave the order, and they slid through the empty streets as though man and car were fresh from the garage. There was not a soul in Portman Square, or a light in any of the houses except the Home Secretary's. They had telephoned through from Stockersham after his departure, and the door opened as he emptied his remaining sovereigns into the chauffeur's hand, before taking Dollar's with no lack of warmth.

"I can't ask you in this time," said Topham Vinson, smiling. "Apart from the hour, I've got to go straight to the telephone, get through to Pentonville, and spoil the Governor's night!"

"Reprieved?" gasped the doctor. It was the one word that would come.

The Home Secretary nodded rather grimly, but was smiling as he shut the door almost on the hand with which John Dollar would have seized his once more. There was a shooting of bolts inside.

Dollar turned slowly round, wondering if at last he could tell the little driver something about the night's enterprise in which he had played so heroic a part. There was no need. The driver had kept eyes and ears wide open—and collapsed once more over the wheel. This time it was not in sleep, but in a dead faint; and the driving goggles were all awry, the driver's hat had tumbled off, the driver's hair had broken bounds.

It was a girl's hair, and the girl was Lady Vera Moyle.

III

A HOPELESS CASE

Alfred Croucher had the refreshing attribute of looking almost as great a ruffian as he really was. His eyes swelled with a vulgar cunning, his mouth was coarse and pitiless; no pedestal of fine raiment could have corrected so low a cast of countenance, or enabled its possessor to pass for a moment as a gentleman or a decent liver. But he had often looked a worse imitation than on the morning of his triumphant exit from the jail, his bullet head diminished in a borrowed cap, his formidable physique tempered by a Burberry all too sober for his taste.

Nor was that all the change in Mr. Croucher at this agreeable crisis of his career. The bulging eyes were glazed with a wonder which quite eclipsed the light of triumph; and they were fixed, in unwilling fascination, upon the tall figure to which the borrowed plumes belonged, whom he had never beheld before that hour, but at whose heels he trotted from the bowels of the prison to the motor-car flashing in the sun beyond the precincts.

"'Alf a mo'!" cried Croucher, making a belated stand instead of jumping in as he was bid. "I didn't rightly catch your name inside, let alone wot you got to do with me an'

my affairs. If you come from my s'lic'tor, I should like to
know why; if you're on the religious lay, 'ere's your 'at an'
coat, and I won't trouble you for a lift."

"My name is Dollar," replied the motorist. "My business
is neither legal nor religious, and it need not necessarily be
medical, though I do happen to be a doctor. I came at the
request of a friend of yours, in that friend's car, to see if
there's nothing we can do to make up to you for all you've
been through."

"A friend of mine!" ejaculated Croucher, with engaging
incredulity.

The doctor smiled, but dryly, as he had spoken. "It's
one of the many unknown friends you have gained lately,
Mr. Croucher. And I should like to make one more, if only
to the extent of a little spin and some breakfast at my house.
There is more sympathy for you than you seem to realize,
and one or two of us are ready to show it in any way you will
permit. But I wouldn't stand here, unless you want a public
demonstration first."

Mr. Croucher decided to disregard the suspicions that
a kindness always excited in his mind, and took his place
in the car without further argument or a second look at the
handful of the curious already collecting on the pavement.
In a moment he was wondering why he had been such a fool
as to hesitate at all. The car slid out of the shadow of the
prison into the sunlight of a bright spring morning, over a

sparkling Thames, and through the early traffic without let or hitch. And the gentleman in the car knew how to hold his tongue, and to submit himself to sidelong inspection as a gentleman should. But little had Croucher made of him by Welbeck Street, except that he looked too knowing to be a crank, and not half soft enough for his notion of the good Samaritan.

Breakfast removed any lingering misgivings, but might have created them in a more sophisticated mind. It was an English breakfast fit for a foreign potentate; there were soles, kidneys, eggs and bacon, hot rolls, and lashings of such coffee as made Mr. Croucher forget a previous craving for alcohol. He thought it funny that so generous a repast should be served on a black old table without a cloth, and he did not fancy the leathern chairs with the great big nails, more fit for a museum than a private gentleman's house. But a subsequent cigar, in which the private gentleman did not join him, was up to the visitor's highest standard, and the subject of a more articulate appreciation than all that had gone before.

"You shall smoke the box if you care to stay with me," said Doctor Dollar, with a warmer smile.

"Stay with you!" exclaimed Croucher, suffering a return of his worst suspicions. "Why should I stay with you?"

"Because there are worse places, Croucher, and one of them has left you a bit of a wreck."

"A bit of one!" cried the other, in a sudden snarling whine. "They've just about done me in, doctor, if you want to know. Two munfs' 'ard, that I was never ordered, on top of one in the condemned cell for what I never done! That's 'ow they've tret me—somefink crool—wuss than wot you'd treat a dawg wot give you 'ydrophobia. And wot *'ad* I done? 'Elped meself when the stuff was under my nose, an' me starvin', an' the jooler's winder ready broke for a cove by them as never 'ad his temptions. I don't say it was right, mind you; but that much I did do, and not what they said I 'ad an' couldn't prove. They couldn't prove it, because I never done it; they couldn't 'ang me, because they didn't dare; but they made me sweat an' shiver just the same. They took ten years off of me life; they give me such a time as I shan't forget till my dying day. And as if that wasn't thick enough, they give me two munfs' 'ard on their own—no judge or jury for that little lot—an' turn me out wot *you* calls a bit of a wreck, but *I* calls a creepin' corpse!"

And the animated remains wiped a forehead wet already with the throes of deglutition, and eyes that were not wet at all, before applying a flickering light to his neglected Upmann.

"What you say is perfectly fair," observed the doctor, in a sadly unimpassioned tone; "but it is also fair to remember that others have been saying it for you for some time past, and that you are free this morning as the result. I confess I feared they might keep you longer; but I evidently had not your grasp of the niceties of your actual offense. As to your mental and bodily sufferings, I can see some of the effects for myself, and those at least I could undo. That was the idea in meeting you, and perhaps I ought to say at once that it was not my idea. It was that of the unknown friend of whom I have already spoken; but I am prepared to carry it out. I run a kind of nursing home, here in my house, and there's a bed ready for you if you care to occupy it."

"A nursing 'ome!" said Croucher, shrinking from a vision of lint and ligatures. "There's nuffunk so much the matter with me that I want to go into an 'ome."

"Nothing that rest could not cure—rest and diet—I agree," said the doctor, with an eye on the empty dishes.

"But won't it cost a lot?" inquired Croucher, thinking of the kidneys especially. "I'm stony-broke, you see," he explained with increased bitterness.

"Our friend insists on paying the bill," said the doctor, grimly.

"And who is our wonderful friend, doctor, when 'e or she's at 'ome?"

Doctor Dollar laughed as he pushed back his chair. "That's the one thing you mustn't ask me; but come up and see the room before you make up your mind against it."

It was at the top and back of the house, less lofty than those into which the Home Secretary had peeped on a previous occasion, but similarly appointed, and more attractive in the morning light and that of a fire already crackling in the grate. By the fireside stood a white wicker chair and a glass table strewn with the newest and lightest of monthly and weekly literature; ash-trays and match-boxes were in comfortable evidence; a bed of vestal purity was turned down in readiness, and a suit of gay pajamas airing with a bathgown on a set of bright brass pipes.

"The bathroom is next door," explained the doctor; "you would have it practically to yourself, but your room would be your castle."

And he pointed out an efficient bolt upon the door.

"You wouldn't lock me in on the other side?" suggested Croucher suspiciously.

"Certainly not; you may have the key; but I should expect you to keep to your own floor, and, of course, to the house. You would not be a prisoner in any sense; but if you went out, Croucher, I'm afraid you would have to stay out. Otherwise my treatment would not have a fair chance; what you require, in the first instance, is absolute rest and no more truck with the outside world than you had where you have been."

"An' good 'olesome grub?" suggested Croucher with another slant of his goggle eyes.

"And plenty of square meals. Perhaps not so square as this morning's, because you won't have any exercise; but that sort of thing."

"A little drop of anythin' to drink, doctor?"

"With your meals, and in moderation, by all means; but don't ask me for nightcaps, and don't try to smuggle anything in."

"I wouldn't do such a thing!" exclaimed Croucher, with virtuous decision. "Doctor, I'm your man, and ready to turn in as soon as ever you like."

And a shabby waistcoat hung unbuttoned at the swoop of a horned thumb.

"One moment," said the doctor. "If you are really coming to me, and coming to stay, I am to telephone to my tailor, who will take some little time getting here."

"Your tailor!" cried Croucher. "Where the dooce does 'e come in?"

"You may well ask!" replied Dollar with involuntary candor. "That friend in need, who was the first to assert your innocence, and to whom you owe more than you will ever know, is anxious to give you a fresh start in life, and an entire new outfit in which to make it."

"Well! I call that 'andsome," declared Alfred Croucher, for once without reserve. "I won't arst 'oo it is no more, but I shall live in 'opes o' findin' out an' sayin' thanky like a man. Not but wot it's right," he added after all, "for them as is rich to 'old out an 'elpin' 'and to them as is pore and 'ave been tret like I've been, through no fault o' their own. But it ain't everybody as sees it like that, an' it makes you think better o' the world when you strike them as does."

"I agree," said the doctor, in a tone entirely lost on his expansive patient.

"I'm griteful to 'im," that worthy went so far as to assert, "and to you too, sir, if it comes to that."

Doctor Dollar took the opportunity of being no less explicit in his turn.

"There's no reason why it should come to that, Croucher, I assure you. I can not too strongly impress on you that anything I do for you is by business arrangement with the friend who takes this extraordinary interest in your career."

In this statement, but especially in its relative clause, there was a note of sheer resentment which recalled other notes and other clauses to the retentive memory of Mr. Croucher. In a flash the lot had fused in his suspicious mind, and so visibly that Dollar was relieved to find himself the object of suspicion.

"You talk as if it went against your grain," said Croucher, with a growl and a show of growler's teeth. "I 'ope you don't think I went an' done it all the time, do yer?"

"I don't follow you, Croucher."

"I mean the big job—the first job—the one I very near swung for!" muttered the fellow, hoarse and hot with evident emotion.

"No; indeed I don't," responded the doctor, in an unexpected voice; and he sighed, as though to think that his sentiments toward his patient should have been so misunderstood.

Such at least was the patient's final interpretation of all that was unsatisfactory in the doctor's manner; and if a doubt still rankled in his mind, it was but the crumpled petal in what was almost literally a bed of roses. Bed and room alike were the most luxurious in which Alfred Croucher had ever lain; after prison they were as the seventh heaven after the most excruciating circle of Dante's Inferno. He stretched his great limbs in peace ineffable, fell asleep dreaming of the fine flash suits for which they had been duly measured, and was never decently awake until the evening.

A substantial tea, when he did wake up, was the least they could provide after neglecting to rouse a man for his midday meal; but a distinct grievance on that score was forgot in the appetite that accrued for dinner, and the infinitely tactful choice of the eventful viands. Steak and onions was the strong act of a romantic drama after the very heart of this transpontine rough. If he had been shown a bill of fare, Alfred Croucher would have chosen steak and onions, with Welsh rarebit to follow; and Welsh rarebit did follow, as if by magic. There was rather less to be said for the drink; the patient could have done with a longer and a stronger draught. But it was a drop of good stuff, if Mr. Croucher was any judge; and he decided not to create a possibly prejudicial impression by complaints of quality or quantity.

"You done me top-'ole," he murmured, rolling his bulbs of eyes when the doctor stood over him once more. "Top-'ole, you 'ave, and no error. I never struck a nicer bit o' fillet. Saucy glass o' wine that, too. Not that I was ever much 'and at the liquor, but there are times w'en it seems to do yer good."

"You shall continue to take it, medicinally," returned Dollar, gravely; "but don't count on the type of fare you've had to-day. Three meals in future, but rather lighter ones. The first day was different, I tried to put myself in your place, and am glad I seem to have succeeded on the whole. But remember you are here to lie low, and that doesn't do on fighting food. Sufficient for the day, Croucher! Here are some flowers from the friend who works by stealth, and these are the weeds I promised you this morning. You might do worse than judge the givers by their gifts."

It was perhaps as well that Alfred Croucher did not pause to puzzle out that saying, for the rare blooms were as pearls before his kindred of the sty, but the box of Upmanns as a trough of offal. One was ignited without delay; yet it was hardly a matter of hours before the chartered sluggard was blissfully asleep once more, his door locked and bolted on principle, and a red fire dying in the grate.

II

It might have been a falling coal that woke him up. Such was the innocent Croucher's first impression. But in that case it was nothing less than a shower of coals, a gentle but continuous downpour, and they fell with a curiously crisp and metallic tinkle. Moreover, the sound was not from the fire after all, but apparently from the window on the opposite side of the room.

Croucher lay listening until his quickened senses could no longer be deceived. Somebody was at his window, the dormer window that anybody could get at over the leads, that ought to have been securely barred but wasn't, as he suddenly remembered with aggrieved dismay. He had himself considered that unprotected window and those conducive leads, in one of his last waking moments, as a not impossible solution of the whisky problem.

But this was different; this was awful; this was a case for alarming the house without scruple or delay. It should have been a great moment for a bit of an expert, who had once served the humane equivalent of seven years for an ambitious burglary of his own; but the defect of character which had spelled failure on that occasion, when an elderly householder had held him up with an unloaded revolver, rendered Mr. Croucher incapable of appreciating the present situation as it deserved. He was far too shaken to think of the former affair, or to feel for a moment like a 'busman on his proverbial holiday or an actor at the front of the house. He did feel bitterly indignant that a patient in a nursing home should be exposed to such terrors by night; and he had got as far as his elbow toward a display of spirit (and incipient virtue) when the catch flew back with as much noise as he might have made himself. Before more could happen, Mr. Croucher had relapsed upon his pillow with a stentorian snore.

Then a sash went up too slowly, limbs crossed the sill and felt the floor with excessive caution, and for a little lifetime Alfred Croucher suffered more exquisitely than toward the end in the condemned cell. The monster was leaning over him, breathing hotly in his face, all but touching his frozen skin.

"Alfie!" said a blessed voice, as a tiny light struck through the compressed eyelids. "Alfie, it's me!"

And once more Alfred Croucher was a man and a liar. "Shoddy!" he croaked with a sepulchral sob. "An' me asleep an' dreamin' like a bloomin' babby! Why, wot the 'ell you doin' 'ere, Shod?"

"Come to see you, old son," said Shoddy. "But it's more like me arskin' what *you're* up to in a 'ouse like this?"

"'Avin the time o' me life!" whispered the excited patient. "Livin' like a fightin' cock, on the fat o' the teemin' land, at some ruddy old josser's expense!"

And he poured into the still adjacent ear the true fairy tale of his first day's freedom, from his introduction to Doctor Dollar in the precincts of that very jail which was to have been his place of execution and obscene sepulcher.

"I know. I seen you come out with him," said Shoddy, "an' drive off in yer car like a hairy lord. I was there with a taxi meself——"

"There to meet me, Shod?"

"That's it. That's 'ow I tracked you to this 'ere 'ouse. The room took more findin'; but there's an old pal o' mine a shover in the mews. 'E showed me the back o' the 'ouse, an' blowed if I didn't spot yer at yer winder first go off!"

"That must've been early on, old man? I bin in bed all day. Oh, such a bed, Shoddy! I'm goin' to sleep me 'ead into a pulp afore I leave it."

"You ain't," said Shoddy firmly. "You're comin' along o' me, Alfie. That's why I'm 'ere."

"Not me," replied Alfie, with equal firmness. "I know w'en I'm well off—and it's time I was."

"I'm wiv yer there!" Shoddy nodded in adroit sympathy; he had kept his electric lamp burning all the time; and an extra prominence of eye and cheek-bone, a looseness of lip and a flickering glance, were not inarticulate in the chastened countenance of his friend. "It must've been 'ell, Alfie, real, old red-'ot 'ell!"

"And all for wot I never done," he was reminded with some stiffness.

"That's it," the other agreed, with perfunctory promptitude. "But that's exactly why I'm 'ere, Alfie. You didn't think I done a job like this for the sake o' tikin' 'old o' yer 'and, didger? It's just because it seems you didn't commit yerself, Alfie, that I'd got to see yer by 'ook or crook before the day was out."

"Where's the fire?" inquired Alfie, idiomatically; but his professional friend, like other artists in narration, and all givers of real news, was not going to surrender the bone of the situation until his audience sat up and begged for it.

Mr. Croucher literally did sit up, while the exasperating Shoddy interrupted himself to make a stealthy tour of the room, in the course of which his electric torch illumined the comfortably bolted door, and the delectable box of Upmanns. To one of these he helped himself without permission, but a brace were in blast before he resumed his position on the bed.

"The fire?" said he, as though seconds and not minutes had elapsed since the cryptic question. "There's no fire anywhere as I know of—not to-night—but there soon may be, that's why I want you out o' this. If you didn't commit yourself, Alfie, don't you see as somebody else must 'ave done?"

"Oh, bring it up!" cried Croucher under his breath.

"Well, if you didn't stiffen that copper on the night o' the sufferygite disturbance—an' we know you didn't—then somebody else did!"

"You don't mean to tell me you know who did?"

There had been a tense though tiny pause; there was another while Shoddy changed the torch to his right hand, and blew a cloud over the head of his now recumbent companion.

"I know what everybody says, Alfie."

"More than their prayers, I'll bet, like they did before. Wot do they say?"

"One o' the sufferygites——"

"Corpsed the copper?"

"That's it, old man."

"And I never thought of it!"

"It bears some thinkin' about, don't it?" said Shoddy. "Why, you're trem'lin' like a blessed leaf!"

"I should think I was trem'lin'! So would you if you'd been through wot I been ... Shod!"

"Yuss, Alfie?"

"I see the 'ole blessed thing!"

"I thought you would."

"It was 'er wot broke the jooler's winder for me!"

"That's wot they say."

"They? Who?"

"Lots o' people. I 'eard it down some mews: some o' the pipers 'ave 'inted at it. Topham's in fair 'ot water all round; they say 'e's 'ushed it up because she's in serciety."

"Wot's 'er nime, Shod?"

"Lidy Moyle—Lidy Vera Moyle, I think it is. And 'ere's another thing, a thing that I was forgettin'."

"Out with it."

"I see 'er come 'ere this afternoon, whilst I was watchin' the 'ouse in case you come out."

"My Gawd, Shoddy! Let me sit up. I can't breathe lyin' down."

"She 'ad some flowers wiv 'er," said Shoddy, pursuing his reminiscences. "Looks as though she's got a friend in the 'ome."

"I'm the friend," said Mr. Croucher grimly. "Take and run yer light over that wash-stand; the guv'nor brought 'em up 'isself wiv these 'ere smokes."

"Roses, in the month o' March!" murmured Shoddy, as a bowl of beauties filled the disk of light; "'ot'ouse flowers for little Alfie! Why, the girl's fair struck on you, cully!"

"I'll strike 'er!" said Alfie, through teeth that chattered with emotion. "I very near 'anged for the little biter, and don't you forget it!"

"Not me," said Shoddy, steering for the bed with his headlights of white-hot filament and red-hot cigar. "That's wot brought me 'ere through thick and thin."

"So she's the great unknown!" said Croucher more than once, but not twice in the same tone. "So it was 'er, was it?" he inquired as often, until Shoddy insisted on a hearing.

"Don't I keep tellin' yer?" said Shoddy. "That's wot brings me, at the gaudiest risks you ever see—only to 'ear you gas! Can't you listen for a change? There's a big thing on if you've guts enough for the job."

It was a simple thing, however, like most big things; the projector had it at his finger-ends; and in a very few minutes Mr. Croucher was considering a complete, crude, and yet eminently practical proposition.

"There's money in it," he was forced to admit, "if there ain't the big money you flatter yerself. But I believe she thinks o' givin' me a start in life any'ow."

"This'd be a start an' a finish, Alfie! Besides, it'd be your revenge; don't you forget wot you've been through," urged the other.

"Catch me!" said Croucher, eagerly. "But—don'cher see? I been through so much that I was lookin' forward to dossin' down 'ere a bit. I ain't the man I was. It's wot I need. Where's the fire, as I said afore? The gal won't run away."

"That's just wot she will, Alfie; goin' abroad any day—an' might get married any day, a piece like 'er. Then you might find it more of a job. There's another 'old we've got, an' might lose any old day."

The other hold appealed with peculiar power to the character and temperament of Alfred Croucher, and not less strongly to a certain sagacity which added more to his equipment. But he had never been quite so comfortable in his life; comfort had never been so decidedly his due; and the substance of present luxury (with a fresh start in the near future) was not lightly to be exchanged for a gold-mine, with all a gold-mine's gambling chances, including the proverbial optimism of prospectors.

The discussion ended in a compromise and the withdrawal of Shoddy by the catlike ways and means of his arrival. But he did not depart without pointing, through the open window and a forest of chimney-stacks, to a lighted but uncurtained square on a lower level. And thither, at certain appointed hours, the patient might have been caught peeping, or even in the act of rude and furtive signals, for several days to come.

Handled as it deserves, the tale of those days would make a psychological chapter of dual interest, and for reasons that may yet appear. But for the moment Alfred Croucher holds the stage, and soliloquies are out of vogue. Yet even his objective life had points of interest. He slept less than he had planned to sleep, but read more than he had ever read in all his life; and his reading, if not a sign of grace, was at least a straw that showed the way the wind might have blown but for the intrusive Shoddy.

Out of the doctor's little typewritten list, the patient in the top-floor-back began by choosing *For the Term of His Natural Life*. It held him—with a tortured brow that sometimes glistened. When the book was finished, he was advised that *It Is Never Too Late to Mend* was a better thing of the same kind; "In spite of its name," added Dollar, in studied disparagement. Croucher took the hint, and was soon breathing as hard as he had done before he knew that Shoddy was Shoddy; was heard blaspheming over Hawes in his solitude, and left wondering what Tom Robinson's creator would have made of Alfred Croucher. Something of that speculation found its way into words, with the return of the book, and was the cause of lengthier visitations from the doctor, whose eye began to brighten when it fell on Croucher, as that of a man put on his mettle after all.

And then one morning he came in with a blue review and a new long poem, which might have hurt but might have helped; only it had no chance of doing either, because the top back room was empty of Alfred Croucher, who had walked out of the house in the loudest of his brand-new clothes.

III

The Rome Express had left Paris sprinkled with the green flakes of a precocious spring; and it hummed through a mellow evening into a night of velvet clasped with a silver moon. The famous train was not uncomfortably crowded; it is not everybody who will pay two pounds, eight shilling, seven pence for a berth in a sleeper which in Switzerland, say, would cost some twenty francs. Most of those who had committed the extravagance seemed by way of getting their money's worth; even the lady traveling alone in the foremost *wagon-lit*, though she refrained from dining in the restaurant-car, would have struck an acquaintance as in better spirits than for some months past. And so she was. But she was still far from being the Lady Vera Moyle of last year's fogs.

She was going to her mother, who had been seriously ill since Christmas, but was now completing her recovery in Rome. And yet her illness had meant less to Lady Armagh than to the wayward child who had been told (by the rest of the family) to consider herself its cause; it might indeed have been a direct dispensation to tie Lady Vera's hands and tongue; and in the *train de luxe*, perhaps for the first time, she herself recognized the merciful wisdom of Providence in the matter.

Alfred Croucher was a free man: that was the great thing. There were moments when it was an even greater thing than Lady Armagh's convalescence. But there was later and greater news yet for Lady Vera to gloat over in the train. Not only was poor Croucher a free man, but that dear Doctor Dollar had hopes of him at last! He had said so the day she left for Paris; he had never said anything of the kind before. Nothing could have been more pessimistic than the crime doctor's first report on his latest patient; nothing franker than the way he had made room for him in the home, merely and entirely to gratify her whim. Alfred Croucher was "not his style," and there had been an end of him but for the fact that Lady Vera was.

She belonged to the class that he was pleased to consider as potentially the most criminal of all. She was well aware of it, and the knowledge provided her with a considerable range of feelings as the train flew on and on. She felt herself the object of a purely pathological interest; she felt almost as small as a specimen under a microscope; she felt lonelier than ever in her life before....

Lonely she was in the way that mattered least. She was traveling for once without a maid. The faithful creature (a would-be militant of the blood-thirstiest, in her day) had been with her dear ladyship over the Sunday in Paris (hobnobbing with certain exiles for the Cause); but just as they were leaving their hotel a telegram had come to summon her to a bucolic death-bed. Esther would have let her old father die without her, but her beloved ladyship, still quick with her own filial awakenings, had sent her about her dismal business with a kiss.

The compartment was overheated; they always are unless you complain in time. Lady Vera had made her efficient little fuss too late, and the result was not apparent before the small hours and Modane. During the long wait there she lay awake, though she had duly entrusted her keys to the conductor, and the voices of those who had omitted that precaution caused a welcome change in her "long, long thoughts." She put her mind to her fellow-passengers, and kept it on them with native resolution.

She was in decent company: a moderately well-known man and wife in one adjoining compartment, a white-haired ecclesiastic in the other. She wove a romance about the venerable gentleman, and speculated on the well-being of the other pair. In such innocent ways could she amuse herself when out of muddle-headed mischief in the name of God knows what. In all else she was sweet and sane enough— unless it was just one tiny matter that annoyed her memory before she fell asleep to the renewed lullaby of the express. It was the utterly unimportant matter of a youngish man in a loud suit, one of a brace of incredibly common Englishmen, who had nevertheless been staying at the hotel in Paris, had "passed a remark" to Esther in the lift, and certainly stared with insolence at Esther's mistress, not only in Paris but in passing along the corridor of this very train, before and after the hour for dinner.

To Vera Moyle there seemed no time at all between her passing thought of this creature and the vile glare that woke her up. At first it blinded her, for she was in the upper berth, within inches of the excruciating blaze. It came almost as a relief when a head bobbed between the glare and her eyes.

Lady Vera blinked her indignation. She was too sleepy to do more at first, and too old a traveler to make much fuss about a mere piece of stupidity. She could not see the man's face, but his head was of the type which occasions the inevitable libel on the bullet, and its hideousness hardly mitigated by the Rembrandtesque effect of the electric light behind it. She conceived it to belong to some blundering official, and ordered him out in pretty sharp French. But the man did not move. And in another short moment Vera Moyle had become aware of three very horrible things: it was the creature in the loud suit, and he had shut the door behind him, and was holding an automatic pistol to her breast.

"One syl'ble that anybody else can 'ear," he muttered as her mouth opened, "an' it's yer larst in life! 'Old yer noise an' I won't be 'ard on you—not 'alf as 'ard as you been on me!"

"It isn't—oh, surely it isn't Croucher?" cried the girl, with an emotion made up of every element but fear.

"It is Croucher," said he in brutal mimicry. "That bein'
just so, I puts away the barker—see?—no decepshun!" The
pistol dropped into a loud tweed pocket. "I reckon I can
do me own bit o' barkin'—yuss! an' bitin', too!" concluded
Croucher, with an appropriate snarl.

"Will you please go out?" said Lady Vera, still with
sorrow in her steady eyes.

"No, I will not please. I'll see you damned first!" said
Croucher, with sudden ferocity—"like you very near seen
me! If we're over'eard, you'll be thought no better'n you
ought to be; but by Gawd they won't think you as bad as
wot you are!"

Lady Vera took no advantage of a studious pause.
The ruffian was making his points with more than merely
ruffianly effect; the whole thing might have been carefully
rehearsed. But to the girl in the upper berth it was now no
more than she deserved. It was a light enough punishment
for the dreadful deed by her committed—no matter how
unconscious, in how fine a frenzy or how just a cause—and
on him visited with all but the last dread vengeance of the
criminal law. He had a right to say what he liked to her after
that, even to say it then and there, with all his natural and
acquired brutality. Was it not she who had done most of all
to brutalize him?

"That is, until I tell 'em," added Croucher, with crafty
significance. His hearer had to recall the words before the

pause; when she had done so, he was again requested to leave the compartment, and there was a harder light in her eyes.

"Surely it isn't Croucher?"

"I'll see you in the morning," she promised. "I'm going on to Rome."

He laughed scornfully. "You needn't tell *me* where you're goin'! I know all about you, and 'ave done for some time. I been on yer tracks, my dear! You seen me. It's your own fault we didn't 'ave it out before. This ain't quite the pitch—but it's a better place than the one you got me into!"

"I got you—out again," was what Lady Vera had begun to say, but something about him made her stop short of that. "I was doing my best for you," she continued humbly. "I thought you were going to let me give you a fresh start in life."

"A fresh start! I want a bit more than that, lidy!"

"Well, what do you want?"

He rolled his eyeballs over the racks laden with her hand-luggage.

"Your jewel-case," said he promptly. "Which is it?"

"That one, in this corner, over my feet."

Her equal alacrity might have been the mere measure of her eagerness to get rid of him; but Alfred Croucher was far too old in deception to be himself very easily deceived.

"Then you can keep it, with my love!" said he. "I'll trouble you for them rings instead—*and* the rest wot you're 'idin' be'ind 'em!"

The girl turned paler in the electric light She was sitting up in her suspicious readiness to point out the jewel-case;

the other hand, with most of her rings on it, had flown instinctively to her throat; for she was traveling, as ladies will, with her greatest treasures—her diamond necklace and pendant, and a string of pearls—on her neck for safety.

"Suppose I refuse and——"

She glanced toward the bell.

"Then I'll say what *I* know."

"And what do you know?" Her back was to the wall.

"What I see that night! What I see an' was mug enough not to twig till I come out an' 'eard all the talk! Is that good enough? If not, the rest'll keep; but it'll put you in the jug all right, I don't care 'oo's on your side. It's one law for the rich and one for the pore. 'Ang me as never done it, an' 'ush you up, as did! But I've heard tell that murder will out, an' you'll find that murderers will in—to prison—even when they're titled lidies with the King on 'is throne be'ind 'em! It'll ruin you, if it does no more—ruin you an' yours—an' break all your 'earts!"

It was enough. She stripped her neck, she stripped her fingers; rings and necklace, pearls and pendant, all lay in a shimmering heap in his capacious palm, held for a moment's triumph under the electric light, reflected for that moment in a mirror which his bulky frame had hidden until now.

It was the mirror on the door of the miniature dressing-room between every two compartments in the *train de luxe*; but in the very moment of his exultation it ceased to reflect either Alfred Croucher or his ill-gotten spoil. The door had opened; it framed a sable figure crowned with silvery locks; lean hands flew out from the black shoulders, and met round the neck of Croucher with the fell dexterity of a professional garroter.

The pair backed together without a word. The one had murder in his set teeth, the other death in the bulging eyes and darkening face, with its collar of interlaced fingers white to the nails with their own pressure. Lady Vera watched the two men as the fawn might watch the python struck to timely death, until the communicating door shut upon them both, and only her own unearthly form remained in the mirror. And the train ran on and on, and the whole coach creaked and trembled, as coaches will even in a *train de luxe*, only in that particular compartment it had not been noticeable for some time.

Presently, as her nerve came back, one or two further observations of a negative order were gradually made by Vera Moyle. She may be said to have noticed that she did not notice one or two things she might have expected to notice by now. The chief thing was that there was no sound whatever from the compartment beyond the looking-glass door, no fuss or undue traffic in the corridor. What had happened? Only too soon she knew.

They had stopped at some nameless station between the tags of the Italian boot. It was a chance of peeping out, and out peeped the shaken girl from her window overlooking the line. And there, skipping on to the next low platform, bag in hand, went the loud trousers under Alfred Croucher's equally new and noisy ulster; and there at his elbow went the venerable ecclesiastic, even holding him by the sleeve!

It was a long road to Rome for Lady Vera Moyle, but toward the end there came another stage in which the *wagon-lit* forgot to swing and sing like humbler coaches, and the pale Campagna swam past unseen. It began with a knock behind the drawn blind of her compartment—now but a mirrored divan of Utrecht velvet and stamped leather—as unsuggestive of a good night's rest as the white face and the bright eyes behind the tiny table in the corner.

"*Entrez!*" she cried with nervous irritation.

The door opened and shut upon the somber face and long athletic limbs of John Dollar.

"Doctor Dollar! I had no idea you were in the train!"

Her voice had broken with very joy; her hand trembled pitifully during its momentary repose in his.

"You have never shown up, you see," said he. "I have been in the next compartment all the way from Paris."

"The next compartment on which side?"

He jerked his head at his own reflection in the looking-glass door.

"But there was a priest in there!" cried the girl.

"There was the high priest of a new religion in which you'll never believe any more," said Dollar with a wry smile. "May he sit down for a minute, Lady Vera?"

She looked at him with cooling eyes. "Certainly, Doctor Dollar, if it makes an explanation any easier."

"I didn't intend to explain at all," he had the nerve to tell her. "I meant my ecclesiastical body to do that for me—but its wig was blown out of the window on the other side of Genoa. I've been hanging about all day in the hope of catching you. I couldn't leave it any longer. I had to give you these."

And he placed upon the table between them the diamond necklace and pendant, the string of pearls, and the handful of rings she had been wearing in the night.

"You made him give them up!" she cried, in thankful tears that never fell, but only softened and sweetened her indescribably.

"Naturally," he laughed. "It wasn't very difficult."

"And I thought you were a confederate when I saw you crossing the line together!"

"I was putting the fear of a foreign jail upon him to the last. But he had a confederate in the train; he was in reserve outside your berth until I lured him into mine and laid him out. Otherwise I should have been with you sooner; but in one way it was better to take our man with your jewels on him—there was no getting out of it. The two of them were only too glad to be kicked out at the first station. And the other fellow was a man who broke into my house to see Croucher the first night we had him there."

"Did they tell you so?"

"No. I knew it at the time. I heard the whole thing, even to fragments of a conversation from which it was possible to reconstruct the plan they actually brought off last night. I make it a rule not to listen at patients' doors, any more than one would at other people's, but I'm not going to blush for this particular exception."

Her soft wet eyes were looking him through and through.

"Yet you kept him on—for my sake!"

"Not altogether, Lady Vera." They were an honest couple. "It put me on my mettle; it gave me something to prevent. At first—as I'm afraid you knew—I really didn't want to touch the fellow with a pole. He was an obvious incurable; he would have been better hanged—justly or unjustly."

"Don't speak of that—or do!" exclaimed the girl. "It makes me forgive him everything!"

"Well, my first idea was about right. He was beyond reclaim. But I never thought he would give me a definite move to block; that, as you know, is one's chief job after all, and it put a new complexion on the case. It was as though— as though one took a man on for cancer and found him plotting to shoot the Chancellor of the Exchequer before he died! I apologize for the analogy, Lady Vera," said Dollar, making the most of their laugh, "but the man became a new proposition on the spot. And the funny thing is that I believe I almost might have cured him after all—done him some good, anyhow—but for the very thing that bucked me up!"

Lady Vera looked out at a flying brake of naked trees, the color of cigar-ash. He had lost her attention for the moment.

"I was a little fool," she said at length. "I should have listened to you, and been content to help in some other way. I am sorry."

"I'm not!" replied Doctor Dollar. "It was a very sporting folly—but everything you ever did was that!"

She shook her head sadly, as a brown river, girt with olives, flashed under the train like a child's skipping-rope.

"I haven't changed my opinions," she said, just a trifle aggressively. "But I would give my life to undo many of my actions—not only that one—many, many!" and she looked him bravely and humbly in the eyes. "So the whole thing has served me right, and will if it happens all over again."

"If what does?"

"This blackmailing of me by that poor man!"

"It won't. I've frightened him."

"He will think of some subtler way."

"There's no subtlety in him, no power, no initiative, no anything but mere brute force," said Dollar, with a touch of that same strength and weakness in his unusually emphatic assertion. "The fellow is a deadly tool and nothing more. He knuckled under to me in a moment."

Lady Vera shook her head again, but this time she was looking firmly in his face.

"I feel," she said, with a stoical conviction, "that I shall be fair game to him as long as we are both in the world. And it's what I deserve."

Dollar abandoned his attempt at disingenuous disabuse; the extreme to which he flew instead was a little startling, but these two knew each other.

"You must marry, Lady Vera," he was moved to say. But his manner was eminently uninspired. He might have been telling her she must hand her keys to the hotel porter at Rome. That was in fact the note he meant to take, only he sang it louder than he knew.

"I can never marry," she answered calmly. "I have blood upon my hands."

"You can marry a man who knows!"

And the unaltered note took on a tremolo of which he was both aware and ashamed; but still their eyes were frankly locked.

"I can marry nobody, Doctor Dollar."

"The man I mean isn't fit to black your boots! But he'd protect you, he'd help you, and you would be the making not only of him but of his dream—and not only *his* little dream——"

It was her hand that stopped him. It had taken his across the little table.

"The man you mean is worth ten million of me! But I can never marry him or anybody. And you, and you alone, know why!"

She bent her brave eyes back on the Campagna; a pale tufted heath was swimming by; gum-trees hardly heightened the prevailing neutral tint; a modern corrugated roof, pinned in place by a few primeval boulders, held her attention on its swift course across the window-panes; and when she looked round, Lady Vera was all alone.

IV

THE GOLDEN KEY

"Shelley was quite right!" exclaimed the young man at the book-shelf, with the prematurely bent back turned upon Doctor Dollar at his old oak desk.

"He was never wrong when he stuck to poetry," said the doctor, looking up from an unfinished prescription on which the ink was nevertheless dry.

The other gave a guilty start. He was an immaculate young wreck, with the fashionable glut of hair plastered back from a good enough face, as if to make the most of its haggard pallor. And he was in full evening dress, for the crime doctor's patients came at all hours.

"Did I say anything?" he asked with exaggerated embarrassment.

"You thought something aloud," said Dollar, smiling. "Don't let it worry you; that's not one of the straws that shows an ill wind. What is it of Shelley's, Mr. Edenborough?"

"Only a bit of one of his letters," said the young man. "I just happened to open them at something that rather appealed to me." And the book shot back into its place.

"Not the bit about the prussic acid, I hope?" suggested the doctor, for all the world as if in fun.

"What was that?" said Edenborough, with a face that would not have imposed upon an infant.

"A little commission from Shelley to Trelawny, for a small quantity of the 'essential oil of bitter almonds,' as he called it, so that he might 'hold in his possession that golden key to the chamber of perpetual peace.'"

"That was it," said the youth at length. "I may as well be honest about it. But I don't know how on earth you knew!"

The doctor gave a kindly little laugh.

"Only by knowing the book," he assured the patient. "It's rather a notorious passage—and you had just been clamoring for at least a silver key to some chamber of temporary peace!"

"You said you would give me one, Doctor Dollar."

"And now I think I won't," said the doctor, rising from his aged chair. "No; you shall not go without hearing my reasons, and what I am going to propose to you instead. These keys, Mr. Edenborough"—and he tore the unfinished prescription into little bits—"gold or silver, they are not keys at all, but burglars' jemmies that injure and vitiate the chambers they break into. It certainly is so with the night's rest you want at any price; it may be the same with the perpetual peace that Shelley took for granted. Yet I happen to have a Chamber of Peace of sorts here in this house. It's my latest fad. You've found it a name, and in return I should like to offer it to you for the night."

"Do you mean a room that sends you off instead of drugs?"

"Did I say anything?"

Young Edenborough was looking puzzled, but for the moment taken out of himself. He had heard of Doctor Dollar as a rather eccentric consultant, but as the very man for him, from no less an authority than the Home Secretary of England, and no further back than that very evening at dinner. He had come straight round from Portman Square, foreseeing miracles and magic potions; but he had not foreseen John Dollar, or his unprofessional conversation, or the slight cast that actually added to his magnetic eyes, his cheery yet gentle confidence, or (least of all) a serious if casual invitation for the night.

"That's exactly what I do mean," said the author of these surprises. "It's the most silent room in London, and there are other little points about it. I got our friend Topham to give it a trial during the bread strike. His verdict was that the Chancellor of the Exchequer would sleep the sleep of the just there!"

Edenborough had a laugh that turned him back into a schoolboy; but he checked it sharply, as though the sound put him to shame and pain.

"I would give anything for one decent night," he said. "But you are far too good, sir, especially to a man you know nothing at all about."

"I ought to know more in the morning, Mr. Edenborough, but it will keep very well till then. Enough for the night that you're a friend of the Home Secretary, and at your worst at just the time when a man wants to be at his best."

Edenborough smote his brow like a young man on the stage, but with a piteous spontaneity beyond all histrionic art.

"It's on Thursday!" he cried, as one in exquisite dread. "My God, I'm to be married on Thursday, and this is Sunday night! How can I toe the mark unless I get some sleep? And how can I sleep——"

"Leave that to me," said Dollar, cutting a pregnant pause as short as possible; "leave everything to me, and come straight up-stairs. I keep the room in constant readiness; you shall be fitted with pajamas, and I'll send a special messenger anywhere you like for whatever you may want in the morning. Come, my dear man! I am burning to give my Chamber of Peace a crucial test, because I know we shall all come out with flying colors!"

There was less confidence in the Doctor Dollar who ran down-stairs a little later and sat at his telephone with an urgent face. In another minute he had left the house, and in another two Mr. Topham Vinson was opening the door to him in Portman Square.

"I call this too bad of you," began the doctor, short of breath and shorter still of patience with his powerful friend.

"My dear fellow, I couldn't help it," vowed the Minister, with disarming meekness. "He would go straight to you, and just then I couldn't have rung you up without giving him away at this end."

"I can stay five minutes," said Dollar, looking at his watch, "to hear as much as you can tell me in the time of what I ought to have known before I saw your neurotic friend."

"Hasn't he told you all about himself?"

"Hardly a word worth anything in a case like this, where the cause matters more than the effect. Of course I could have insisted, but that might have finished him off for the night. I gather, however, that he's one of the First Lord's secretaries, but a friend of yours, on the brink of being married, and in more than the normal state about it, or something to do with it."

"I'll take your points in order," said Topham Vinson, who could be brisker than anybody when he chose. "George Edenborough is not only one of Stockton's secretaries, but the most private and most confidential of the crowd. I don't know about his being a friend of mine; I've been a friend to him for family reasons, and found him a nice enough fellow. But the girl he's going to marry—if they do marry—is one of us."

"If!" cried the doctor. "Do you mean to say she'd draw back in the last week?"

"She may not be able to help herself," was the grave reply. "George Edenborough is under a cloud that may burst at any moment."

"A sudden cloud?"

"Out of the blue for me. I only heard of it from Stockton on Friday night. But it's no new thing to him. He might have told me sooner, I think, seeing it was through me that Edenborough ever went to him."

"In some special capacity, I rather gather?"

"Yes; he can draw a bit—in fact, he's not a secretary at all except in name, but the First Lord's private draftsman. Stockton's a whale for details but a dunce at technicalities. What he likes is the thing on paper, as he sees it with his own eyes; so he makes his inspections with Edenborough and a sketch-block, illustrated notes are taken at every turn, and all sorts of impossible improvements worked out in subsequent collaboration. I had that this evening from the boy himself. It will show you what chances he has had of giving things away—or—selling them!"

"Is it as bad as that?"

"Stockton swears it is. To me it's inconceivable. But he gives chapter and verse of at least one drawing that found its way across the North Sea early in the year. Edenborough admits that he either lost it or had it stolen from him. He seems to have been more careful—whichever way you look at it—during the summer. But this autumn the trouble has begun again. A dockyard sketch-map has flown the German Ocean, come home to roost by some means into which we'd better not inquire, and is pronounced by Stockton a bad imitation of one made for him by Edenborough six weeks ago."

"Why a bad imitation, I wonder?"

"The original has been in the First Lord's archives ever since; he says the copy must have been made from memory; but he has good reasons why nobody but Edenborough could have made it."

"Reasons that are not so good in law, apparently?"

"Exactly; as yet there's no case and there has been no accusation. But I very much fear that traps are being set, and I've taken it on myself to put the madman on his guard."

"To-night?"

"Yes; it was the first chance of getting hold of him, and that only by having the poor little bride to dinner as well. Heavy work, Dollar, drinking their healths and knowing what was in the air! The only comfort was that Edenborough knew as well as I did; it was written on his face, if you had the key, and I hadn't to do much beating about the bush when I got him to myself. He was wonderfully frank, from his point of view. He told me that the air of suspicion was driving him out of his mind; he said he hadn't slept for nights and nights."

"Although no accusation has been made?"

"Although not an open word has been said to connect him with the bad copy of his own map!"

"That's the worst thing you've told me," said Dollar quietly. "He protested his innocence, of course?"

"In absolute tears!"

"And what was your own impression, Mr. Vinson?"

"Extremely mixed. I felt that he was speaking the truth, and yet not the whole truth. He had an air of guilty knowledge, if not of actual guilt."

"His physical condition bears you out," observed the doctor with reluctance. "And the poor devil's to be married in four days' time!"

"There my pity's on the other side."

"But the girl's another friend of yours? May I ask her name?"

"Lucy Trevellyn."

"Any relation of Admiral Trevellyn?"

"Own daughter to the old sea-dog, and if anything the breezier of the two! I couldn't imagine a young girl more like an old salt at heart. She'd go to sea if she could; as she can't, she's a little pillar of the Navy League—and engaged to the First Lord's best young man! Could you conceive a more ingenious irony, or a greater tragedy when the truth comes out? Dollar, it must come out before Thursday, if it's ever coming out at all!"

"Is it otherwise a likely match?"

"The very likeliest, but for this world's goods, and there'll be more of them one day. She has go enough for two, and they have tastes in common. I told you he could draw a bit, but she's a little artist, though you wouldn't think it if you saw her teaching him to skate at Prince's or taking me on at golf! Lucy Trevellyn's the best type of sportswoman—just as Vera Moyle is one gone wrong."

John Dollar was on his feet.

"Well, I've stayed longer than I intended," said he abruptly. "I promised to go up within half an hour to see if he was asleep. And he will be. But what's a night's rest against such a tragedy as the whole thing's bound to be!"

"Or such a mystery?" suggested Topham Vinson. "If you could only get to the bottom of that, Dollar, we might know how to act."

"I'm not a detective," returned the doctor—but the stiff words were hardly out before the stiff lips relaxed in a smile. "I've said that before, Vinson, and I shouldn't wonder if you made me say it again. I am out to stop things happening, not to bother about things that have been done and can't be mended. But in this case discovery may be the mother of prevention, and I must have a shot with both barrels while there's time."

He had come in glum and grumbling; he went off gay and incisive, subtly enlivened by the very gravity of the matter, as he always was. But it was grave enough, as was Dollar himself behind the sparkling mask that he wore unawares in all times of stress. And on one point his confidence was justified without delay; the young man in the Chamber of Peace was found drenched already in slumbers worthy of the name he had unwittingly bestowed upon that magic fastness.

But this was not a case in which the crime doctor could leave well alone. Every hour of the night he was up-stairs and down again; and, in the intervals, either deep in such grim reading as the Illustrative Cases of Transitory Mania, in the terrible fourth volume of *Casper's Forensic Medicine*, or deeper yet in his own cognate speculations.

In the morning it was he who carried up the patient's suit-case, woke him up, and watched the rising tide of memory drown the thanks in his throat. Now was the doctor's chance of checking Mr. Vinson's version of the young man's troubles; but he waited for George Edenborough to open his own heart, and waited in vain till the last five minutes, when the boy began to thank him and ended with the whole story.

It differed very little from the second-hand synopsis, but it confirmed more than one impression which Dollar would have given much to relinquish. The talk of intolerable suspicions was indeed more consistent with a guilty conscience than anything else, since it was duly followed by the admission that nobody had expressed such suspicions in anything like so many words. The crime doctor was sorry he had put the question; it was the only one he asked. But by exhorting Edenborough to get all the exercise he could, and by saying he had heard great things of Miss Trevellyn's skating, the reluctant dissembler had little difficulty in obtaining an immediate invitation to tea at Prince's Skating Club.

Edenborough had departed with a face almost radiant at the prospect; yet he had scarcely spoken of his beloved until the subject of skating cropped up. It was as though that was the only relation in which he could still think of her without pain and shame; and in due course he was discovered on the ice with the same look of lingering pride and joy.

It was the height of the skating afternoon, and the glassy strip an opaque pane on which a little giant might have been scribbling with a big diamond. The eye swam with pairs rotating as in a circus—with single practitioners at work under dashing instructors down the middle of the rink—while the ear sang with a resounding swish of skates. One of the workers was George Edenborough, who came off one leg, with a glistening forehead, to find his guest a good place behind the barrier.

"So glad you're not late for the waltzing," he said nervily. "I've had a long day out of town, and didn't get here myself till much later than I expected. Lucy's writing a letter in the lounge, but she'll be here in a minute for the enclosure, and after that we'll have tea."

Dollar ascertained that the waltzing enclosure was a close quarter-of-an-hour for all but those more or less proficient in that delicate and astounding art. Edenborough said that he himself was not quite up to the standard of these displays, and suited the action to the word by taking the floor unsteadily on his skates. As he seated himself a gong sounded, the band struck up, beginners dispersed, confident hands clasped lissome waists, long edges ended in lightning threes, and the rink was a maze of sweeping grace and symmetry.

Dollar had never seen anything like it in his life, for artificial ice was in its infancy in London before the war, and ever since he had been a busy man. He followed first one couple and then another, and each seemed to him more competent and graceful than the last. Yet the first short waltz was not over before an involuntary selection had eliminated all but a dark strong girl in red and a swarthy man with bright eyes and a black mustache.

"Those two are the best," said he—"that girl in red and the heavy alien."

"Do you think so?" cried the delighted Edenborough. "Then you're a judge, because that's Lucy!"

"I didn't mean to insult her partner," said Dollar in some dismay. "He's the best waltzer on the ice except Miss Trevellyn."

"He's an Italian marquis," returned Edenborough, in another voice. "Rocchi's his beastly name. I've no use for the fellow. But he can skate."

The first waltz finished there were two more in quick succession, and Edenborough had a better word for Miss Trevellyn's next partner. He was only a glowing schoolboy, home from Eton for his leave, but the past mistress lent herself to his dash and fling with a gusto equal to his own.

"I'm glad that's over," said Edenborough, as she escaped with her life from the desperado's clutches. "I say, confound that fellow Rocchi!"

She was waltzing with the handsome brute again; for he looked no less, with his deep blue chin and insolent eyes, and his air of conscious mastery. Edenborough plainly loathed him, chafing visibly as the pair swept past with certainly the appearance of some extra verve for his benefit. Dollar himself was very disagreebly impressed, and that down to the end, when Rocchi skated up with the lady, whom he surrendered with a gleam of palpable bravado.

Yet that impression altered with the very opening of Miss Trevellyn's not less resolute mouth. She had good teeth and a hearty voice, and eyes of a breezy and humane audacity. Dollar thought of Topham Vinson's tribute, and agreed with all except the odious comparison. There was, indeed, no comparing types as different as Lucy Trevellyn and Vera Moyle; but the one had never puzzled him in the past more completely than did the other before he took his leave.

And they had talked about the wedding, and their presents, and the wedding trip, as though neither God nor man could interfere!

"Only three days to go!" said Dollar to himself. And two of the three were soon gone without alarums or excursions, except on the part of the crime doctor himself. He was neglecting his practise for the case in hand; he was nowhere to be found when badly wanted on the Tuesday night, nor yet on the Wednesday morning; and this was the more extraordinary in that it was George Edenborough who wanted him, now with an ashier face than ever, and now on the telephone in a frantic voice.

At dusk on the Wednesday his key turned in the latch, and next day's bridegroom burst from the waiting-room at the same moment.

"At last!" cried Edenborough; and looked so ghastly in the electric light that Dollar did not switch it on in the consulting-room, or ask a question as he shut the door.

It was one of those mild unseasonable days on which the best of servants keep up the biggest fires; the doctor opened the French window that led from his den, down rusty steps, into a foul and futile enclosure of grimy gravel and moribund shrubs. In the meantime Edenborough had not taken a seat as mechanically bidden, but had planted himself in defiant pose before the fire; and the glow showed restless hands twitching into fists, but not the face of which one look had been enough.

"You might have left word where you were!" he began with great bitterness.

"I have just done so," returned Dollar, "at your rooms. I was wanting to see you—presently. It seems like fate, to find you here before me."

"I suppose you've heard the latest, wherever you've been?" pursued Edenborough, aware and jealous of some independent perplexity on the part of Dollar.

"I have heard so much!" said the doctor, dropping into a chair. "Better be explicit—and as expeditious as you can, my dear fellow. I have an appointment almost directly."

"Oh! there's not much to say," rejoined the other sardonically. "You remember when you came to Prince's, doctor?"

"I do, indeed."

They both spoke as if it were weeks ago.

"You know I told you I'd had a hard day out of town?"

"I remember."

"I meant with my chief—Lord Stockton—seeing his new brood of submarines."

"In their unfledged state, I suppose?"

"That was it—and making the usual sketches. That's my job—or was! I was Stockton's walking Kodak until yesterday afternoon; then I got the boot for a wedding present, and a chance of the jug for my honeymoon!"

The harsh voice broke, for all its sudden slang and satire. Dollar was driven to his only policy.

"I'm not going to pretend I don't know of this," he said. "I know of it from the Home Secretary. A duplicate of one of those last drawings of yours——"

"A duplicate!"

"Well, a bad imitation, if you like."

The doctor paused as though he had finished a sentence, as though the amended phrase had interrupted his thought.

"Well?" said Edenborough grimly. "Did you hear how they got hold of it?"

"Intercepted in the post, I gathered, on its way abroad."

"In our post," said Edenborough. "Almost a *casus belli* in itself, I should have thought!"

"And have you no idea how it came there?" asked the doctor bluntly—but now he meant to be blunt; he was not sorry when his man flew into a feeble passion on the spot.

"What the devil do you mean, Doctor Dollar? I know no more about the matter than—I was going to say, than you do—but I begin to think you know more than you pretend!"

"I didn't think I had pretended," said Dollar, simply.

"Well, what *do* you know?" demanded Edenborough, in a fury of suspicion. "All, I suppose?" he added, with a schoolboy sneer, when the answer was slow to come.

"Yes; all," said the doctor, very gravely and reluctantly, as though driven into a pronouncement of life or death.

There was no outcry of surprise from Edenborough. He had some pride. But his knees began to tremble in the firelight, and his unclenched hands to twitch.

"I don't believe it," he exclaimed at length. "You tell me what you know!"

"All that you yourself suspected, and made yourself ill with suspecting—and couldn't sleep for suspecting—long ago!"

Pitiful tone and tender hand carried a heavier conviction than the words. And now it was the patient who had sunk into the chair, the doctor bending over his bowed and quivering shoulders.

"Mark my words closely"

"You are not the first man, my dear Edenborough," he went on, "who would seem to have been betrayed in cold blood by a woman—by *the* woman. Mark my words closely. I say it seems so. I would not condemn the greatest malefactor unheard. I meant to hear Miss Trevellyn first—feeling in my bones, against all reason, that there may still be some unimaginable explanation. But, if the worst be true of her, then the best is true of you; for you are the first man I have known bear the brunt as you have borne it, my very dear fellow!"

"What makes you suspect her?" groaned Edenborough to the ground.

"It's not a case of suspicion—don't deceive yourself as to that, Edenborough. I *know* that Miss Trevellyn produced—and parted with—those last two sketches about which there's been all the trouble. I only *suspect* that she got you to show her the originals, almost as soon as they were made, on the plea of her tremendous interest in the Navy."

"Quite true; she did," said Edenborough, but as though he did not appreciate what he was saying, as though something else had stuck in his mind. "But it *was* a tremendous interest!" he exclaimed, jumping up. "It was her father's interest; his life, indeed! Isn't it inconceivable that his daughter—apart from everything else I've found her—that she of all people should do a thing like this?"

"I am afraid the inconceivable happens almost as often as the unexpected," said Dollar, with a sigh. "Criminology, indeed, prepares us for little else. Think of the perfectly good mothers who have flown to infanticide as the first relief of a mind unhinged! The inversion of the ruling passions is one of the sure symptoms of insanity."

"But of course she's mad," cried Edenborough, "if she's guilty at all. But that's what I can't and won't believe. I can believe it one minute but not the next, just as I've suspected and laughed at my suspicions all this nightmare time. One look in her face has always been enough, and would be at this minute."

"Well, we shall soon see," said Dollar, glancing at the clock. "But I can only warn you that my evidence is overwhelming."

"Let's have it, then; what is your evidence?" demanded Edenborough, in a fresh fit of stone-blind defiance.

"My dear fellow, you force my hand!" said Dollar. "God knows you have a right—and it can't make matters worse than they are. My evidence consists of a full and circumstantial confession by a scoundrel to whom I took your own dislike at sight, and whose career I have spent the week investigating. I needn't tell you I mean the infamous Rocchi."

"Rocchi!" whispered Edenborough at the second attempt, as though his very tongue rejected the abhorrent name. Yet now he stood perfectly still, like a man who sees at last. "Well," he added in an ominously rational voice, "I must live long enough to send *him* to hell, whatever else I do."

"You will have to find him first," said Dollar. "He has gone back to his paymasters—not his own countrymen—they kicked him out long ago. I've taken it on myself to do the same, instead of handing him over to the police and doing an infinite deal more harm than good."

But Edenborough was not listening to a word; he was talking to himself, and he talked aloud as soon as he was given a chance.

"Now we know why she was so keen on my wretched job ... on the whole Navy?... No, not a life-long fraud like that.... And she pretended to dislike that brute as much as I did! I believe she did, too, but for his waltzing.... No, never jealous of him, and I'm not now ... but so much the worse, so much the more damnably cold-blooded!"

Dying philosopher could not have displayed a more acute detachment. But the last touch was lost upon Dollar, whose expectant ear had caught the ting of an electric bell.

"Edenborough," he said, in the voice of urgent conciliation, "the time has come for you to show what's in you. So far you have kept your head and played the man; keep it now, and you will play the hero! I still can't imagine what Miss Trevellyn can have to say for herself—but I implore you to hear her out, for I believe she is being admitted at this moment."

"Lucy—here—and you expected her?"

"I told you I had another appointment. But you were here first, one thing led to another, and it may be better as it is. You were bound to have this out between you—and to-day. If you wish me to be present—but no human being can help!"

"Unless it's you!" suggested Edenborough in a panic-stricken whisper. "I can't face her alone—I can't trust myself!"

Dollar took no notice of a knock at the door. "Edenborough, you must," he said gently; "and whatever she may have to say—much or little, and it may be much—you must hear patiently to the end. It's your duty, man! Don't flinch from it, for God's sake!"

"But I do flinch from it!" cried Edenborough below his breath. "I flinch from it for her sake as much as mine. I'm not the one to shame her, even if Rocchi's telling——"

The door opened in response to Dollar's decisive call. It was the little Barton boy, to say that Miss Trevellyn was in the waiting-room.

"Show her in," said Dollar. "I have more than Rocchi's bare word, Edenborough."

The distracted youth looked about him like a wild creature in a cage, and saw his loophole at the last moment.

"I won't be the one to shame her, whatever she has done!" he whimpered through his teeth. "If there's any explanation, she need never know I knew; if there's not, good-by!"

And he slipped through the open window, out upon the iron steps, as Dollar switched on the lights that turned the outer dusk to darkness; and the door opened even as the curtain was drawn in desperation, with a last signal to Edenborough to stand his ground and at least hear all.

"Good evening, Doctor Dollar," said Miss Trevellyn, briskly, and with that she stopped in her sturdy stride. "Is anything the matter?"

"Is it possible you don't know what?"

"Is it anything to do with George? You're his doctor, aren't you?" These questions quicker, but with a sensible check on any premature anxiety.

"He has consulted me, but the matter more directly concerns yourself. It's no use beating about the bush, Miss Trevellyn!" exclaimed the doctor, with a sudden irritation at her straight carriage and straighter look. "I have to speak to you about the Marchese Rocchi."

"Have you, indeed!"

Miss Trevellyn had winced at the name, but already her eyes looked brighter and bolder, and the firm face almost serenely obdurate.

"The Marchese Rocchi," he continued, "fled the country yesterday, Miss Trevellyn."

"I wondered why he was not at Prince's!"

"He fled because of a scandal in which you are implicated," said Dollar very sternly. "He has been trafficking in naval secrets—this country's secrets, Miss Trevellyn—and he swears you sold them to him. Is it true?"

"One moment," said the girl, with a first trace of emotion. "Is all this of your own accord, or on behalf of Mr. Edenborough?"

"Of my own accord entirely."

"You've been ferreting things out for yourself, have you?"

"You are entitled to put it so."

"Detective as well as doctor, it appears?"

"Miss Trevellyn, I implore you to tell me if these things are true!"

"So that you may tell your patient, I suppose?"

"No. I shall not tell him," said Dollar, disingenuously enough, but with the deeper sorrow.

"Very well! I'll tell you, and you can shout it from the roof for all I care now. It's perfectly true!"

Dollar started, not at the thing that had to come, but at the manner in which it came. It seemed, indeed, the last word in wickedness—impenitent, unblushing, even vainglorious to eye and ear alike. His glance flew to the curtained window, but no sound or movement came from the iron stair outside.

"True that you sold those drawings to this man Rocchi?" he heard himself saying at last, in a tone so childish that he scarcely wondered at the smile it drew.

"Perfectly true," said Miss Trevellyn.

"Drawings made by George Edenborough for the First Lord of the Admiralty, and shown to you because you were the stronger character and insisted on seeing them, but only in such confidence as might almost be justified between future man and wife?"

"I didn't sell his drawings," said Miss Trevellyn, impatiently. "I copied them, more or less from memory, and sold my own efforts."

"Of course I know that! It was a slip of the tongue," he admonished her, while marveling more and more. "And you can put the whole thing plainly without so much as a blush!"

"I am going to put you to the blush instead, Doctor Dollar," returned the lady, with a lighter touch. "You are very clever at finding out what I did, but you don't ask why I did it; that's not so clever of such a clever man, and I must just enlighten you before I go. The first drawing was not a copy; it was the original they got that time, and it was stolen from Mr. Edenborough on his way home from the Admiralty. He never knew exactly where it was stolen, but I always thought I knew. You are a bit of a detective, Doctor Dollar; well, so am I in my way. You have not let me into the secret of your success, and I shouldn't think of boring you with mine. I thought it happened at Prince's, and I suspected Rocchi, that was all. It was last spring, and I had all the summer to think about it. But when Prince's opened I set to work, for there was Rocchi making up to us both as before. He didn't get much change out of George, but perhaps I made amends when George wasn't there, and sometimes even when he was! He could waltz, you see, and so can I," said Lucy Trevellyn, with something like a sigh for her bereavement on the rink.

"Yet you copied the other two drawings, and you even admit you sold him the copies?"

"I sold them quite well," said Miss Trevellyn, with sparkling eyes—"and you may guess what I did with the money—but it's not fair to call them copies. I made them as inaccurate as possible without spoiling everything, and indeed I couldn't have made them very accurate from memory, and they were only rough sketches to begin with! Of course George was wrong to let me see them, but he was assisting in the best of causes. Rocchi was an expert professional spy. I soon sized him down as one. But he was not a naval expert—and I'm that as well! That's my last boast, Doctor Dollar; but it's not unjustifiable, if you come to think of George and me between us keeping a national enemy out of serious mischief, feeding a friendly Power with false plans, and giving the money to our own dear Navy League!"

Dollar surveyed the radiant minx with eyes that needed rubbing. His only sorrow was that Edenborough did not burst through the curtains without more ado; he must have extraordinary self-control, when he liked.

"Not that George was a conscious party to the fraud; he wouldn't have approved of it, he couldn't possibly, poor George!" said George's bride. "But I shall tell him all about it now; of course I always meant to tell him—after to-morrow—but he has had quite enough bothers of his own, and this was my show. I suppose you don't know what's been bothering him, Doctor Dollar? He says it's overwork, and I do think Lord Stockton's an old slave-driver; do you know, I haven't even seen George since the day before yesterday at Prince's?"

"Nor I," said Dollar, no longer with the least compunction, "from that hour to this."

"Of course I know he's all right," concluded Miss Trevellyn, as they were parting perfect friends, "because he has rung me up several times to say so, and he looked better on Monday than for ever so long. But I must own I shall be glad when I get him away for a real good rest."

She had refused to hear another word from Dollar in explanation, or of regret, and she made her departure with all the abruptness of a constitutionally decided person. But she had blushed once at least in the last few minutes. And the doctor ran back into his den with singing heart, ready to fall upon his patient's neck in deep thanksgiving and even more profound congratulation.

No patient was there to meet him even now, but the curtain swayed a little before the open window. Dollar reached it at a bound; but there was nobody outside on the iron steps, and the curtain filled behind him as the inner door banged in the draft. The horrid little space at the back of the house, between the high black walls with the broken-bottle coping, lay empty of all life in the plentiful light from the back windows—but for an early cat that fled before Dollar's precipitate descent into the basement.

"The gentleman's gone," said Mrs. Barton at once. "He come through this way some time ago—said he couldn't wait no longer out there!"

"How long do you suppose he had waited?"

"Not long," said Mrs. Barton firmly. "Bob here was at his tea when he had to go up to show the young lady in; and the young gentleman, it couldn't've been more than three or four minutes before he was through 'ere as if something had 'appened."

"I didn't hear him."

"He was anxious you shouldn't be disturbed, sir."

"Did you show him out, Bobby?"

The master had never been so short with them. Mrs. Barton felt that something was the matter, but Bobby quaked.

"Yes, sir!"

"Which way did he go—and how—foot or taxi?"

"I—please, sir—I never stopped to see, sir!"

Dollar flew to his telephone; forsook it for a taxicab; drew Edenborough's rooms in vain; inquired as vainly (as an anonymous wedding guest, uncertain of the church) at Admiral Trevellyn's; was at the House of Commons by half past six, and at Scotland Yard (armed with written injunctions from the Secretary of State) before seven.

At that hour and place the matter passed out of the hands of Doctor John Dollar, who could only hasten home to Welbeck Street, there to enter upon the most shattering vigil of his life—the terrible telephone at his elbow—and still more terrible inquirers on the telephone as the night wore on!

But never one word of news.

Toward midnight Topham Vinson arrived with the elaborate sandwiches and even the champagne that he had found awaiting him at home. It was the measure of a born leader; the doctor had not broken his fast since lunch; and in the small hours he once dozed for some minutes in his chair.

But the politician had not the temperament to wait for the telephone to talk to him; he talked repeatedly into the telephone, set a round dozen of myrmidons by the ears, and at last was rightly served by being sent off to Hammersmith to identify the dead body of a defaulting clerk, just recovered from the Thames.

"I'm not coming with you," Dollar had said, even when the description seemed to tally. "Edenborough wouldn't drown himself—and this is my place."

It was a being ten years older who opened his own front door again at daybreak. His face was as gray as the wintry dawn, the whole man bowed and broken. Topham Vinson stood aghast on the step.

"It isn't all over, is it?"

The doctor nodded with compressed lips.

"When and where?"

"I don't know. Come in. They're getting up down-stairs; there'll be some tea in a minute."

"For God's sake tell me what you've heard!"

"Haven't I told you? They rang up just after you went. He bought prussic acid yesterday!"

Dollar had dropped into his elaborate old chair; the bent head between his hands drooped over its own reflection in the monastic writing-table.

"Who rang up?" asked the man on his legs.

"Some of your people."

"Was that all they had to tell you?"

"That was all; we shan't have long to wait for the rest."

"Where did he buy it?"

"At his own chemist's—'to put a poor old dog out of its misery!' His very words, Vinson, so they tell me! I shall hear them all my life."

"And it has taken all night to learn this, has it, from the chemist's where the poor devil dealt!"

Dollar understood this outburst of truculent emotion.

"That was my fault," said he. "I told them to confine their attention to entries made in the poison books after five o'clock yesterday afternoon. Edenborough had signed his name and got the stuff earlier in the day."

"Before you told him anything?"

"He had his own suspicions, you must remember. I had confirmed them—and *her* first words left no more to be said, that he could bear to hear! If only he had waited another minute! If only I had dragged him back to face it out!" groaned Dollar, in a bottomless pit of self-reproach. "I call myself a crime doctor, yet I let my patient creep into space with a bottle of prussic acid, and commit the one crime I had to prevent!"

"Why prussic acid, I wonder?"

The idle question was not asked for information, but it happened to be one that Dollar could answer, and it brought him to his book-shelves with a certain alacrity.

"I know," he said, "though I never thought of it till this minute! I was trying to write him a prescription on Sunday night, when the poor chap suddenly remarked that Shelley was right, and I found him dipping into these Letters, and had the luck to spot the very bit he'd struck. It was this"— and he read out the passage beginning: "You, of course, enter into society at Leghorn: should you meet with any scientific person, capable of preparing the *Prussic Acid, or essential oil of bitter almonds*, I should regard it as a great kindness if you could procure me a small quantity"—down to "it would be a comfort to me to hold in my hands that golden key to the chamber of perpetual peace."

Topham Vinson's only comment was to pick up the book, which had fallen to the floor with the concluding words. Dollar was swaying where he stood, glancing in horror toward the door; at that moment it opened, and Mrs. Barton entered with the tea-tray.

"Mrs. Barton," said the doctor, in a voice that failed him as it had not done all night, "I don't want to hurt your feelings, but did that boy of yours speak the truth when he told me he had seen Mr. Edenborough out?"

"He did not, sir, and his father thrashed him for it!" cried the good woman. "And that was very wrong of Barton, because I was as bad as the boy, in not telling you at the time. So we've all done wrong together, and we don't deserve to stay, as I told the both of them!"

The poor soul was forgiven and consoled, with an unconscious sympathy not lost on Topham Vinson, to whom it was extended a moment later.

"Take a drink of your tea," said Dollar. "It will do you good."

"What about you?"

"I'm going up-stairs first."

"You've thought of something!"

"I have," replied Dollar in a tragic whisper. "I've thought of my 'chamber of perpetual peace.'"

That sanctuary was on the second floor, and it had triple doors so spaced that each could be shut in turn before the next was opened. The house might have been in an uproar, and yet one might have entered this room without admitting the slightest sound by the door. The window was of triple glass that would have deadened an explosion on its sill, and the walls were thickly wadded behind an inner paneling of aromatic pine.

The first sensation on entering was one of ineffable peace and quiet; next came a subtle, soothing scent, as of all the spices of Arabia; and lastly a surprising sense of scientific ventilation, as though the four sound-proof walls were yet not impervious to the outer air, but as though it were the pungent air of pine-clad mountains, in miraculous circulation here in the heart of London.

All this would have struck the visitor by degrees; but to John Dollar, who had devised and superintended every detail, it all came home together and afresh as he entered softly with the Home Secretary; and a certain composite effect, unforeseen in the beginning and still unexplained, fell upon him even now, and with it all the weight of his own fatigue; so that he could have flung himself on bed or couch as a doomed wretch sinks into the snow, but for the light in the room and what the light revealed.

It was light of a warm, strange, coppery shade, that he had found for himself by dyeing frosted electric lamps as children dye Easter eggs; it was the very softest and yet least sensuous shade that eyes ever penetrated with perfect ease, and it turned the room into a little hall of bronze. The simple curtains might have been golden lace, richly tarnished with age; the furniture solid copper; the bed an Eastern divan, and the form upon the bed a sleeping Arab.

It was George Edenborough lying there in all his clothes, a girl's photograph beside him on the coverlet, and beside the photograph a tiny phial that caught the light.

"Stay where you are!" whispered Dollar in a voice that thrilled his companion to the core. And he stole to the bed, stooped over it for a little lifetime, and so came stealing back.

"How long has he been dead?" said Topham Vinson, harshly; but in realty his blood was freezing at an unearthly smile in that unearthly light.

"Dead?" was the doctor's husky echo. "Don't you know the smell of bitter almonds, and have you smelt it yet? Here's the golden bottle he hadn't opened when he lay down—perhaps for the first time since he was here on Sunday night—and this is his wedding morning, and he's only—only fast asleep!"

V

A SCHOOLMASTER ABROAD

It is a small world that flocks to Switzerland for the Christmas holidays. It is also a world largely composed of that particular class which really did provide Doctor Dollar with the majority of his cases. He was therefore not surprised, on the night of his arrival at the great Excelsior Hotel, in Winterwald, to feel a diffident touch on the shoulder, and to look round upon the sunburned blushes of a quite recent patient.

George Edenborough had taken Winterwald on his wedding trip, and nothing would suit him and his nut-brown bride but for the doctor to join them at their table. It was a slightly embarrassing invitation, but there was good reason for not persisting in a first refusal. And the bride carried the situation with a breezy vitality, while her groom chose a wine worthy of the occasion, and the newcomer explained that he had arrived by the afternoon train, but had not come straight to the hotel.

"Then you won't have heard of our great excitement," said Mrs. Edenborough, "and I'm afraid you won't like it when you do!"

"If you mean the strychnine affair," returned Dollar, with a certain deliberation, "I heard one version before I had been in the place an hour. I can't say that I did like it. But I should be interested to know what you both think about it all."

Edenborough returned the wine-list to the waiter with sepulchral injunctions.

"Are you telling him about our medical scandal?" he inquired briskly of the bride. "My dear doctor, it'll make your professional hair stand on end! Here's the local practitioner been prescribing strychnine pills warranted to kill in twenty minutes!"

"So I hear," said the crime doctor, dryly.

"The poor brute has been frightfully overworked," continued Edenborough, in deference to a more phlegmatic front than he had expected of the British faculty. "They say he was up two whole nights last week; he seems to be the only doctor in the place, and the hotels are full of fellows doing their level best to lay themselves out. We've had two concussions of the brain and one complicated fracture this very week. Still, to go and give your patient a hundred times more strychnine than you intended——"

And he stopped himself, as though the subject, which he had taken up with a purely nervous zest, was rather near home after all.

"But what about his patient?" adroitly inquired the doctor. "If half that one hears is true, he wouldn't have been much loss."

"Not much, I'm afraid," said Lucy Edenborough, with the air of a Roman matron turning down her thumbs.

"He's a fellow who was at my private school, just barely twenty-one, and making an absolute fool of himself," exclaimed Edenborough, touching his glass. "It's an awful pity. He used to be such a nice little chap, Jack Laverick."

"He was nice enough when he was out here a year ago," the bride admitted, "and he's still a sportsman. He won half the toboggan races last season, and took it all delightfully; he's quite another person now, and gives himself absurd airs on top of everything else. Still, I shall expect Mr. Laverick either to sweep the board or break his neck. He evidently wasn't born to be poisoned."

"Did he come to grief last year, Mrs. Edenborough?"

"He only nearly had one of his ears cut off, in a spill on the ice-run. So they said; but he was tobogganing again next day."

"Doctor Alt looked after him all right then, I hear," added Edenborough, as the champagne arrived. "But I only wish *you* could take the fellow in hand! He really used to be a decent chap, but it would take even you all your time to make him one again, Doctor Dollar."

The crime doctor smiled as he raised his glass and returned compliments across the bubbles. It was the smile of a man with bigger fish to fry. Yet it was he who came back to the subject of young Laverick, asking if he had not a tutor or somebody to look after him, and what the man meant by not doing his job.

In an instant both the Edenboroughs had turned upon their friend. Poor Mr. Scarth was not to blame! Poor Mr. Scarth, it appeared, had been a master at the preparatory school at which Jack Laverick and George Edenborough had been boys. He was a splendid fellow, and very popular in the hotel, but there was nothing but sympathy with him in the matter under discussion. His charge was of age, and in a position to send him off at any moment, as indeed he was always threatening in his cups. But there again there was a special difficulty: one cup was more than enough for Jack Laverick, whose weak head for wine was the only excuse for him.

"Yet there was nothing of the kind last year," said Mrs. Edenborough, in a reversionary voice; "at least, one never heard of it And that makes it all the harder on poor Mr. Scarth."

Dollar declared that he was burning to meet the unfortunate gentleman; the couple exchanged glances, and he was told to wait till after the concert, at which he had better sit with them. Was there a concert? His face lengthened at the prospect, and the bride's eyes sparkled at his expense. She would not hear of his shirking it, but went so far as to cut dinner short in order to obtain good seats. She was one of those young women who have both a will and a way with them, and Dollar soon found himself securely penned in the gallery of an ambitious ballroom with a stage at the other end.

The concert came up to his most sardonic expectations, and he resigned himself to a boredom only intensified by the behavior of some crude humorists in the rows behind. Indifferent song followed indifferent song, and each earned a more vociferous encore from those gay young gods. A not unknown novelist told dialect stories of purely territorial interest; a lady recited with astounding spirit; another fiddled, no less courageously; but the back rows of the gallery were quite out of hand when a black-avised gentleman took the stage, and had not opened his mouth before those back rows were rows of Satan's reproving sin and clapping with unsophisticated gusto.

"Who's this!" asked Dollar, instantly aware of the change behind him. But even Lucy Edenborough would only answer, "Hush, doctor!" as she bent forward with shining eyes. And certainly a hairpin could not have been dropped unheard before the dark performer relieved the tension by plunging into a scene from *Pickwick*.

It was the scene of Mr. Jingle's monologue on the Rochester coach—and the immortal nonsense was inimitably given. Yet nobody could have been less like the emaciated prototype than this tall tanned man, with the short black mustache, and the flashing teeth that bit off every word with ineffable snap and point.

"Mother—tall lady, eating sandwiches—forgot the arch—crash—knock—children look round—mother's head off—sandwich in her hand—no mouth to put it in——" and his own grim one only added to the fun and swelled the roar.

He waited darkly for them to stop, the wilful absence of any amusement on his side enormously increasing that of the audience. But when it came to the episode of Donna Christina and the stomach-pump, with the culminating discovery of Don Bolaro Fizzgig in the main pipe of the public fountain, the guffaws of half the house eventually drew from the other half the supreme compliment of exasperated demands for silence. Mrs. George Edenborough was one of the loudest offenders. George himself had to wipe his eyes. And the crime doctor had forgot that there was such a thing as crime.

"That chap's a genius!" he exclaimed, when a double encore had been satisfied by further and smaller doses of Mr. Jingle, artfully held in reserve. "But who is he, Mrs. Edenborough?"

"Poor Mr. Scarth!" crowed the bride, brimming over with triumphant fun.

But the doctor's mirth was at an end.

"That the fellow who can't manage a bit of a boy, when he can hold an audience like this in the hollow of his hand?"

And at first he looked as though he could not believe it, and then all at once as though he could. But by this time the Edenboroughs were urging Scarth's poverty in earnest, and Dollar could only say that he wanted to meet him more than ever.

The wish was not to be gratified without a further side-light and a fresh surprise. As George and the doctor were repairing to the billiard-room, before the conclusion of the lengthy program, they found a group of backs upon the threshold, and a ribald uproar in full swing within. One voice was in the ascendent, and it was sadly indistinct; but it was also the voice of the vanquished, belching querulous futilities. The cold steel thrusts of an autocratic Jingle cut it shorter and shorter. It ceased altogether, and the men in the doorway made way for Mr. Scarth, as he hurried a disheveled youth off the scene in the most approved constabulatory manner.

"Does it often happen, George?" Dollar's arm had slipped through his former patient's as they slowly followed at their distance.

"Most nights, I'm afraid."

"And does Scarth always do what he likes with him—afterward?"

"Always; he's the sort of fellow who can do what he likes with most people," declared the young man, missing the point. "You should have seen him at the last concert, when those fools behind us behaved even worse than to-night! It wasn't his turn, but he came out and put them right in about a second, and had us all laughing the next! It was just the same at school; everybody was afraid of Mostyn Scarth, boys and men alike; and so is Jack Laverick still—in spite of being of age and having the money-bags—as you saw for yourself just now."

"Yet he lets this sort of thing happen continually?"

"It's pretty difficult to prevent. A glass about does it, as I told you, and you can't be at a fellow's elbow all the time in a place like this. But some of Jack's old pals have had a go at him. Do you know what they've done? They've taken away his Old Etonian tie, and quite right too!"

"And there was nothing of all this last year?"

"So Lucy says. I wasn't here. Mrs. Laverick was, by the way; she may have made the difference. But being his own master seems to have sent him to the dogs altogether. Scarth's the only person to pull him up, unless—unless you'd take him on, doctor! You—you've pulled harder cases out of the fire, you know!"

They had been sitting a few minutes in the lounge. Nobody was very near them; the young man's face was alight and his eyes were shining. Dollar took him by the arm once more, and they went together to the lift.

"In any case I must make friends with your friend Scarth," said he. "Do you happen to know his number?"

Edenborough did—it was 144—but he seemed dubious as to another doctor's reception after the tragedy that might have happened in the adjoining room.

"Hadn't I better introduce you in the morning?" he suggested with much deference in the lift. "I—I hate repeating things—but I want you to like each other, and I heard Scarth say he was fed up with doctors!"

This one smiled.

"I don't wonder at it."

"Yet it wasn't Mostyn Scarth who gave Doctor Alt away."

"No?"

Edenborough shook his head as they left the lift together. "No, doctor. It was the chemist here, a chap called Schickel; but for him Jack Laverick would be a dead man; and but for him again, nobody need ever have heard of his narrow shave. He spotted the mistake, and then started all the gossip."

"I know," said the doctor, nodding.

"But it was a terrible mistake! Decigrams instead of milligrams, so I heard. Just a hundred times too much strychnine in each pill."

"You are quite right," said John Dollar quietly. "I have the prescription in my pocket."

"*You* have, doctor?"

"Don't be angry with me, my dear fellow! I told you I had heard one version of the whole thing. It was Alt's. He's an old friend—but you wouldn't have said a word about him if I had told you that at first—and I still don't want it generally known."

"You can trust me, doctor, after all you've done for me."

"Well, Alt once did more for me. I want to do something for him, that's all."

And his knuckles still ached from the young man's grip as they rapped smartly at the door of No. 144.

II

It was opened a few inches by Mostyn Scarth. His raiment was still at concert pitch, but his face even darker than it had been as the crime doctor saw it last.

"May I ask who you are and what you want?" he demanded—not at all in the manner of Mr. Jingle—rather in the voice that most people would have raised.

"My name's Dollar and I'm a doctor."

The self-announcement, pat as a polysyllable, had a foreseen effect only minimized by the precautionary confidence of Doctor Dollar's manner.

"Thanks very much. I've had about enough of doctors."

And the door was shutting when the intruder got in a word like a wedge.

"Exactly!"

Scarth frowned through a chink just wide enough to show both his eyes. It was the intruder's tone that held his hand.

"What does that mean?" he demanded with more control.

"That I want to see you about the other doctor—this German fellow," returned Dollar, against the grain. But the studious phrase admitted him.

"Well, don't raise your voice," said Scarth, lowering his own as he shut the door softly behind them. "I believe I saw you down-stairs outside the bar. So I need only explain that I've just got my bright young man off to sleep, on the other side of those folding-doors."

Dollar could not help wondering whether the other room was as good as Scarth's, which was much bigger and better appointed than his own. But he sat down at the oval table under the electrolier, and came abruptly to his point.

"About that prescription," he began, and straightway produced it from his pocket.

"Well, what about it?" the other queried, but only keenly, as he sat down at the table, too.

"Doctor Alt is a very old friend of mine, Mr. Scarth."

Mostyn Scarth exhibited the slight but immediate change of front due from gentleman to gentleman on the strength of such a statement. His grim eyes softened with a certain sympathy; but the accession left his gravity the more pronounced.

"He is not only a friend," continued Dollar, "but the cleverest and best man I know in my profession. I don't speak from mere loyalty; he was my own doctor before he was my friend. Mr. Scarth, he saved more than my life when every head in Harley Street had been shaken over my case. All the baronets gave me up; but chance or fate brought me here, and this little unknown man performed the miracle they shirked, and made a new man of me off his own bat. I wanted him to come to London and make his fortune; but his work was here, he wouldn't leave it; and here I find him under a sorry cloud. Can you wonder at my wanting to step in and speak up for him, Mr. Scarth?"

"On the contrary, I know exactly how you must feel, and am very glad you have spoken," rejoined Mostyn Scarth, cordially enough in all the circumstances of the case. "But the cloud is none of my making, Doctor Dollar, though

I naturally feel rather strongly about the matter. But for Schickel, the chemist, I might be seeing a coffin to England at this moment! He's the man who found out the mistake, and has since made all the mischief."

"Are you sure it was a mistake, Mr. Scarth?" asked Dollar quietly.

"What else?" cried the other, in blank astonishment. "Even Schickel has never suggested that Doctor Alt was trying to commit a murder!"

"Even Schickel!" repeated Dollar, with a sharp significance. "Are you suggesting that there's no love lost between him and Alt?"

"I was not, indeed." Scarth seemed still astonished. "No. That never occurred to me for a moment."

"Yet it's a small place, and you know what small places are. Would one man be likely to spread a thing like this against another if there were no bad blood between them?"

Scarth could not say. The thing happened to be true, and it made such a justifiable sensation. He was none the less frankly interested in the suggestion. It was as though he had a tantalizing glimmer of the crime doctor's meaning. Their heads were closer together across the end of the table, their eyes joined in mutual probation.

"Can I trust you with my own idea, Mr. Scarth?"

"That's for you to decide, Doctor Dollar."

"I shall not breathe it to another soul—not even to Alt himself—till I am sure."

"You may trust me, doctor. I don't know what's coming, but I shan't give it away."

"Then I shall trust you even to the extent of contradicting what I just said. I *am* sure—between ourselves—that the prescription now in my hands is a clever forgery!"

Scarth held out his hand for it. A less deliberate announcement might have given him a more satisfactory surprise; but he could not have looked more incredulous than he did, or subjected Dollar to a cooler scrutiny.

"A forgery with what object, Doctor Dollar?"

"That I don't pretend to say. I merely state the fact—in confidence. You have your eyes upon a flagrant forgery."

Scarth raised them twinkling. "My dear Doctor Dollar, I saw him write it out myself!"

"Are you quite sure?"

"Absolutely, doctor! This lad, Jack Laverick, is a pretty handful; without a doctor to frighten him from time to time, I couldn't cope with him at all. His people are in despair about him—but that's another matter. I was only going to say that I took him to Doctor Alt myself, and this is the prescription they refused to make up. Schickel may have a spite against Alt, as you suggest, but if he's a forger I can only say he doesn't look the part."

"The only looks I go by," said the crime doctor, "are those of the little document in your hand."

"It's on Alt's paper."

"Anybody could get hold of that."

"But you suggest that Alt and Schickel have been on bad terms?"

"That's a better point, Mr. Scarth, that's a much better point," said Dollar, smiling and then ceasing to smile as he produced a magnifying-lens. "Allow me to switch on the electric standard, and do me the favor of examining that handwriting with this loop; it's not very strong, but the best I could get here at the photographer's shop."

"It's certainly not strong enough to show anything fishy, to my inexperience," said Scarth, on a sufficiently close inspection.

"Now look at this one."

Dollar had produced a second prescription from the same pocket as before. At first sight they seemed identical.

"Is this another forgery?" inquired Scarth, with a first faint trace of irony.

"No. That's the correct prescription, rewritten by Alt at my request, as he is positive he wrote it originally."

"I see now. There are two more noughts mixed up with the other hieroglyphs."

"They happen to make all the difference between life and death," said Dollar gravely. "Yet they are not by any means the only difference here."

"I can see no other, I must confess." And Scarth raised his eyes just as Dollar's fell from his broad brown brow.

"The other difference is, Mr. Scarth, that the prescription with the strychnine in deadly decigrams has been drawn backward instead of being written forward."

Scarth's stare ended in a smile.

"Do you mind saying all that again, Doctor Dollar?"

"I'll elaborate it. The genuine prescription has been written in the ordinary way—*currente calamo*. But forgeries are not written in the ordinary way, much less with running pens; the best of them are written backward, or rather they are *drawn upside down*. Try to copy writing as writing, and your own will automatically creep in and spoil it; draw it upside down and wrong way on, as a mere meaningless scroll, and your own formation of the letters doesn't influence you, because you are not forming letters at all. You are drawing from a copy, Mr. Scarth."

"You mean that I'm deriving valuable information from a handwriting expert," cried Scarth, with another laugh.

"There are no such experts," returned Dollar, a little coldly. "It's all a mere matter of observation, open to everybody with eyes to see. But this happens to be an old forger's trick; try it for yourself, as I have, and you'll be surprised to see how much there is in it."

"I must," said Scarth. "But I can't conceive how you can tell that it has been played in this case."

"No? Look at the start, 'Herr Laverick,' and at the finish, 'Doctor Alt.' You would expect to see plenty of ink in the 'Herr,' wouldn't you? Still plenty in the 'Laverick,' I think, but now less and less until the pen is filled again. In the correct prescription, written at my request to-day, you will find that this is so. In the forgery the progression is precisely the reverse; the *t* in 'Alt' is full of ink, but you will find less and less till the next dip in the middle of the word 'Mahlzeit' in the line above. The forger, of course, dips oftener than the man with the running pen."

Scarth bent in silence over the lens, his dark face screwed awry. Suddenly he pushed back his chair.

"It's wonderful!" he cried softly. "I see everything you say. Doctor Dollar, you have converted me completely to your view. I should like you to allow me to convert the hotel."

"Not yet," said Dollar, rising, "if at all as to the actual facts of the case. It's no use making bad worse, Mr. Scarth, or taking a dirty trick too seriously. It isn't as though the forgery had been committed with a view to murdering your young Laverick."

"I never dreamed of thinking that it was!"

"You are quite right, Mr. Scarth. It doesn't bear thinking about. Of course, any murderer ingenious enough to concoct such a thing would have been far too clever to drop out *two* noughts; he would have been content to change the milligrams into centigrams, and risk a recovery. No sane chemist would have dispensed the pills in decimals. But we are getting off the facts, and I promised to meet Doctor Alt on his last round. If I may tell him, in vague terms, that you at least think there may have been some mistake, other than the culpable one that has been laid at his door, I shall go away less uneasy about my unwarrantable intrusion than I can assure you I was in making it."

It was strange how the balance of personality had shifted during an interview which Scarth himself was now eager to extend. He had no longer the mesmeric martinet who had tamed an unruly audience at sight; the last of Mr. Jingle's snap had long been in abeyance. And yet there was just one more suggestion of that immortal, in the rather dilapidated trunk from which the swarthy exquisite now produced a bottle of whisky, very properly locked up out of Laverick's reach. And weakness of will could not be imputed to the young man who induced John Dollar to cement their acquaintance with a thimbleful.

III

It was early morning in the same week; the crime doctor lay brooding over the most complicated case that had yet come his way. More precisely it was two cases, but so closely related that it took a strong mind to consider them apart, a stronger will to confine each to the solitary brain-cell that it deserved. Yet the case of young Laverick was not only much the simpler of the two, but infinitely the more congenial to John Dollar, and not the one most on his nerves.

It was too simple altogether. A year ago the boy had been all right, wild only as a tobogganer, lucky to have got off with a few stitches in his ear. Dollar heard all about that business from Doctor Alt, and only too much about Jack Laverick's subsequent record from other informants. It was worthy of the Welbeck Street confessional. His career at Oxford had come to a sudden ignominious end. He had forfeited his motoring license for habitually driving to the public danger, and on the last occasion had barely escaped imprisonment for his condition at the wheel. He had caused his own mother to say advisedly that she would "sooner see him in his coffin than going on in this dreadful way"; in writing she had said it, for Scarth had shown the letter addressed to him as her "last and only hope" for Jack; and yet even Scarth was powerless to prevent that son of Belial from getting "flown with insolence and wine" more nights than not. Even last night it had happened, at the masked ball, on the eve of this morning's races! Whose fault would it be if he killed himself on the ice-run after all?

Dollar writhed as he thought upon this case; yet it was not the case that had brought him out from England, not the reason of his staying out longer than he had dreamed of doing when Alt's telegram arrived. It was not, indeed, about Jack Laverick that poor Alt had telegraphed at all. And yet between them what a job they could have made of the unfortunate youth!

It was Dollar's own case over again—yet he had not been called in—neither of them had!

Nevertheless, when all was said that could be said to himself, or even to Alt—who did not quite agree—Laverick's was much the less serious matter; and John Dollar had turned upon the other side, and was grappling afresh with the other case, when his door opened violently without a knock, and an agitated voice spoke his name.

"It's me—Edenborough," it continued in a hurried whisper. "I want you to get into some clothes and come up to the ice-run as quick as possible!"

"Why? What has happened?" asked the doctor, jumping out of bed as Edenborough drew the curtains.

"Nothing yet. I hope nothing will——"

"But something has!" interrupted the doctor. "What's the matter with your eye?"

"I'll tell you as you dress, only be as quick as you can. Did you forget it was the toboggan races this morning? They're having them at eight instead of nine, because of the sun, and it's ten to eight now. Couldn't you get into some knickerbockers and stick a sweater over all the rest? That's what I've done—wish I'd come to you first. They'll *want* a doctor if we don't make haste!"

"I wish you'd tell me about your eye," said Dollar, already in his stockings.

"My eye's all right," returned Edenborough, going to the glass. "No, by jove, it's blacker than I thought, and my head's still singing like a kettle. I shouldn't have thought Laverick could hit so hard—drunk *or* sober."

"That madman?" cried Dollar, looking up from his laces. "I thought he turned in early for once in a way?"

"He was up early, anyhow," said Edenborough, grimly; "but I'll tell you the whole thing as we go up to the run, and I don't much mind who hears me. He's a worse hat even than we thought. I caught him tampering with the toboggans at five o'clock this morning!"

"Which toboggans?"

"One of the lot they keep in a shed just under our window, at the back of the hotel. I was lying awake and I heard something. It was like a sort of filing, as if somebody was breaking in somewhere. I got up and looked out, and thought I saw a light. Lucy was fast asleep; she is still, by the way, and doesn't know a thing."

"I'm ready," said Dollar. "Go on when we get outside."

It was a very pale blue morning, not a scintilla of sunlight in the valley, neither shine nor shadow upon clambering forest or overhanging rocks. Somewhere behind their jagged peaks the sun must have risen, but as yet no snowy facet winked the news to Winterwald, and the softer summits lost all character against a sky only less white than themselves.

The village street presented no difficulties to Edenborough's gouties and the doctor's nails; but there were other people in it, and voices travel in a frost over silent snow. On the frozen path between the snow-fields, beyond the village, nails were not enough, and the novice depending upon them stumbled and slid as the elaborated climax of Edenborough's experience induced even more speed.

"It was him all right—try the edge, doctor, it's less slippy. It was that young brute in his domino, as if he'd never been to bed at all, and me in my dressing-gown not properly awake. We should have looked a funny pair in—have my arm, doctor."

"Thanks, George."

"But his electric lamp was the only light. He didn't attempt to put it out. 'Just tuning up my toboggan,' he whispered. 'Come and have a look.' I didn't and don't believe it was his own toboggan; it was probably that Captain

Strong's, he's his most dangerous rival; but, as I tell you, I was just going to look when the young brute hit me full in the face without a moment's warning. I went over like an ox, but I think the back of my head must have hit something. There was daylight in the place when I opened the only eye I could."

"Had he locked you in?"

"No; he was too fly for that; but I simply couldn't move till I heard voices coming, and then I only crawled behind a stack of garden chairs and things. It was Strong and another fellow—they did curse to find the whole place open! I nearly showed up and told my tale, only I wanted to tell you first."

"I'm glad you have, George."

"I knew your interest in the fellow—besides, I thought it was a case for you," said George Edenborough simply. "But it kept me prisoner till the last of the toboggans had been taken out—I only hope it hasn't made us too late!"

His next breath was a devout thanksgiving, as a fold in the glistening slopes showed the top of the ice-run, and a group of men in sweaters standing out against the fir-trees on the crest. They seemed to be standing very still. Some had their padded elbows lifted as though they were shading their eyes. But there was no sign of a toboggan starting, no sound of one in the invisible crevice of the run. And now man after man detached himself from the group, and came leaping down the subsidiary snow-track meant only for ascent.

But John Dollar and George Edenborough did not see all of this. A yet more ominous figure had appeared in their own path, had grown into Mostyn Scarth, and stood wildly beckoning to them both.

"It's Jack!" he shouted across the snow. "He's had a smash—self and toboggan—flaw in a runner. I'm afraid he's broken his leg."

"Only his leg!" cried Dollar, but not with the least accent of relief. The tone made Edenborough wince behind him, and Scarth in front look round. It was as though even the crime doctor thought Jack Laverick better dead.

He lay on a litter of overcoats, the hub of a wheel of men that broke of itself before the first doctor on the scene. He was not even insensible, neither was he uttering moan or groan; but his white lips were drawn away from his set teeth, and his left leg had an odd look of being no more a part of him than its envelope of knickerbocker and stocking.

"It's a bu'st, doctor, I'm afraid," the boy ground out as Dollar knelt in the snow. "Hurting? A bit—but I can stick it."

Courage was the one quality he had not lost during the last year; nobody could have shown more during the slow and excruciating progress to the village, on a bobsleigh carried by four stumbling men; everybody was whispering about it. Everybody but the crime doctor, who headed the little procession with a face in keeping with the tone which had made Edenborough wince and Scarth look round.

The complex case of the night—this urgent one—both were forgot in Dollar's own case of years ago. He was back again in another Winterwald, another world. It was no longer a land of Christmas-trees growing out of mountains of Christmas cake; the snow melted before his mind's eye; he was hugging the shadows in a street of toy-houses yielding resin to an August sun, between green slopes combed with dark pines, under a sky of intolerable blue. And he was in despair; all Harley Street could or would do nothing for him. And then—and then—some forgotten ache or pain had taken him to the little man—the great man—down this very turning to the left, in the little wooden house tucked away behind the shops.

How he remembered every landmark—the handrail down the slope—the little porch—the bare stairs, his own ladder between death and life—the stark surgery with its uncompromising appliances in full view! And now at last he was there with such another case as his own—the minor case that he had yet burned to bring there—and there was Alt to receive them in the same white jacket and with the same simple countenance as of old!

They might have taken him on to the hotel, as Scarth indeed urged strongly; but the boy himself was against another yard, though otherwise a hero to the end.

"Chloroform?" he cried faintly. "Can't I have my beastly leg set without chloroform? You're not going to have it off, are you? I can stick anything short of that."

The two doctors retired for the further consideration of a point on which they themselves were not of one mind.

"It's the chance of our lives, and the one chance for him," urged Dollar vehemently. "It isn't as if it were such a dangerous operation, and I'll take sole responsibility."

"But I am not sure you have been right," demurred the other. "He has not even had concussion, a year ago. It has been only the ear."

"There's a lump behind it still. Everything dates from when it happened; there's some pressure somewhere that has made another being of him. It's a much simpler case than mine, and you cured me. Alt, if you had seen how his own mother wrote about him, you would be the very last man to hesitate!"

"It is better to have her consent."

"No—nobody's—the boy himself need never know. There's a young bride here who'll nurse him like an angel and hold her tongue till doomsday. She and her husband may be in the secret, but not another soul!"

And when Jack Laverick came out of chloroform, to feel a frosty tickling under the tabernacle of bedclothes in which his broken bone was as the Ark, the sensation was less uncomfortable than he expected. But that of a dull deep pain in the head drew his first complaint, as an item not in the estimate.

"What's my head all bandaged up for?" he demanded, fingering the turban on the pillow.

"Didn't you know it was broken, too?" said Lucy Edenborough gravely. "I expect your leg hurt so much more that you never noticed it!"

IV

Ten days later Mostyn Scarth called at Doctor Alt's, to ask if he mightn't see Jack at last. He had behaved extremely well about the whole affair; others in his position might easily have made trouble. But there had been no concealment of the fact that injuries were not confined to the broken leg, and the mere seat of the additional mischief was enough for a man of sense. It is not the really strong who love to display their power. Scarth not only accepted the situation, but voluntarily conducted the correspondence which kept poor Mrs. Laverick at half Europe's length over the critical period. He had merely stipulated to be the first to see the convalescent, and he took it as well as ever when Dollar shook his head once more.

"It's not our fault this time, Mr. Scarth. You must blame the sex that is privileged to change its mind. Mrs. Laverick has arrived without a word of warning. She is with her son at this moment, and you'll be glad to hear that she thinks she finds him an absolutely changed character—or, rather, what he was before he ever saw Winterwald a year ago. I may say that this seems more or less the patient's own impression about himself."

"Glad!" cried Scarth, who for the moment had seemed rather staggered. "I'm more than glad; I'm profoundly relieved! It doesn't matter now whether I see Jack or not. Do you mind giving him these magazines and papers, with my love? I am thankful that my responsibility's at an end."

"The same with me," returned the crime doctor. "I shall go back to my work in London with a better conscience than I had when I left it—with something accomplished—something undone that wanted undoing."

He smiled at Scarth across the flap of an unpretentious table, on which lay the literary offering in all its glory of green and yellow wrappers; and Scarth looked up without a trace of pique, but with an answering twinkle in his own dark eyes.

"Alt exalted—restored to favor—Jack reformed character—born again—forger forgot—forging ahead, eh?"

It was his best Mr. Jingle manner; indeed, a wonderfully ready and ruthless travesty of his own performance on the night of Dollar's arrival. And that kindred critic enjoyed it none the less for a second strain of irony, which he could not but take to himself.

"I have not forgot anybody, Mr. Scarth."

"But have you discovered who did the forgery?"

"I always knew."

"Have you tackled him?"

"Days ago!"

Scarth looked astounded. "And what's to happen to him, doctor?"

"I don't know." The doctor gave a characteristic shrug. "It's not my job; as it was, I'd done all the detective business, which I loathe."

"I remember," cried Scarth. "I shall never forget the way you went through that prescription, as though you had been looking over the blighter's shoulder! Not an expert—modest fellow—pride that apes!"

And again Dollar had to laugh at the way Mr. Jingle wagged his head, in spite of the same slightly caustic undercurrent as before.

"That was the easiest part of it," he answered, "although you make me blush to say so. The hard part was what reviewers of novels call the 'motivation.'"

"But you had that in Schickel's spite against Alt."

"It was never quite strong enough to please me."

"Then what was the motive, doctor?"

"Young Laverick's death."

"Nonsense!"

"I wish it were, Mr. Scarth."

"But who is there in Winterwald who could wish to compass such a thing?"

"There were more than two thousand visitors over Christmas, I understand," was the only reply.

It would not do for Mostyn Scarth. He looked less than politely incredulous, if not less shocked and rather more indignant than he need have looked. But the whole idea was a reflection upon his care of the unhappy youth. And he said so in other words, which resembled those of Mr. Jingle only in their stiff staccato brevity.

"Talk about 'motivation'!—I thank you, doctor, for that word—but I should thank you even more to show me the thing itself in your theory. And what a way to kill a fellow! What a roundabout, risky way!"

"It was such a good forgery," observed the doctor, "that even Alt himself could hardly swear that it was one."

"Is *he* your man?" asked Scarth, in a sudden whisper, leaning forward with lighted eyes.

The crime doctor smiled enigmatically. "It's perhaps just as lucky for him, Scarth, that at least he could have had nothing to do with the second attempt upon his patient's life."

"What second attempt?"

"The hand that forged the prescription, Scarth, with intent to poison young Laverick, was the one that also filed the flaw in his toboggan, in the hope of breaking his neck."

"My dear doctor," exclaimed Mostyn Scarth, with a pained shake of the head, "this is stark, staring madness!"

"I only hope it was—in the would-be murderer," rejoined Dollar gravely. "But he had a lot of method; he even did his bit of filing—a burglar couldn't have done it better—in the domino Jack Laverick had just taken off!"

"How do you know he had taken it off? How do you know the whole job wasn't one of Jack's drunken tricks?"

"What whole job?"

"The one you're talking about—the alleged tampering with his toboggan," replied Scarth, impatiently.

"Oh! I only thought you meant something more." Dollar made a pause. "Don't you feel it rather hot in here, Scarth?"

"Do you know, I do!" confessed the visitor, as though it were Dollar's house and breeding had forbidden him to volunteer the remark. "It's the heat of this stove, with the window shut. Thanks so much, doctor!"

And he wiped his strong, brown, beautifully shaven face; it was one of those that require shaving more than once a day, yet it was always glossy from the razor; and he burnished it afresh with a silk handkerchief that would have passed through a packing-needle's eye.

"And what are you really doing about this—monster?" he resumed, as who should accept the monster's existence for the sake of argument.

"Nothing, Scarth."

"Nothing? You intend to do nothing at all?"

Scarth had started, for the first time; but he started to his feet, while he was about it, as though in overpowering disgust.

"Not if he keeps out of England," replied the crime doctor, who had also risen. "I wonder if he's sane enough for that?"

Their four eyes met in a protracted scrutiny, without a flicker on either side.

"What I am wondering," said Scarth deliberately, "is whether this Frankenstein effort of yours exists outside your own imagination, Doctor Dollar."

"Oh! he exists all right," declared the doctor. "But I am charitable enough to suppose him mad—in spite of his method *and* his motive."

"Did he tell you what that was?" asked Scarth with a sneer.

"No; but Jack did. He seems to have been in the man's power—under his influence—to an extraordinary degree.

He had even left him a wicked sum in a will made since he came of age. I needn't tell you that he has now made another, revoking——"

"No, you need not!" cried Mostyn Scarth, turning livid at the last moment. "I've heard about enough of your mares' nests and mythical monsters. I wish you good morning, and a more credulous audience next time."

"That I can count upon," returned the doctor at the door. "There's no saying what they won't believe—at Scotland Yard!"

VI

ONE POSSESSED

Lieutenant-General Neville Dysone, R.E., V.C., was the first really eminent person to consult the crime doctor by regular appointment in the proper hours. Quite apart from the feat of arms which had earned him the most coveted of all distinctions, the gigantic General, deep-chested and erect, virile in every silver-woven hair of his upright head, filled the tiny stage in Welbeck Street and dwarfed its antique properties, as no being had done before. And yet his voice was tender and even tremulous with the pathetic presage of a heartbreak under all.

"Doctor Dollar," he began at once, "I have come to see you about the most tragic secret that a man can have. I would shoot myself for saying what I have to say, did I not know that a patient's confidence is sacred to any member of your profession—perhaps especially to an alienist?"

"I hope we are all alike as to that," returned Dollar, gently. He was used to these sad openings.

"I ought not to have said it; but it hardly is my secret, that's why I feel such a cur!" exclaimed the General, taking his handkerchief to a fine forehead and remarkably fresh complexion, as if to wipe away its noble flush. "Your patient,

I devoutly hope, will be my poor wife, who really seems to me to be almost losing her reason"—but with that the husband quite lost his voice.

"Perhaps we can find it for her," said Dollar, despising the pert professional optimism that told almost like a shot "It is a thing more often mislaid than really lost."

And the last of the other's weakness was finally overcome. A few weighty questions, lightly asked and simply answered, and he was master of a robust address, in which an occasional impediment only did further credit to his delicacy.

"No. I should say it was entirely a development of the last few months," declared the General emphatically. "There was nothing of the kind in our twenty-odd years of India, nor yet in the first year after I retired. All this—this trouble has come since I bought my house in the pine country. It's called Valsugana, as you see on my card; but it wasn't before we went there. We gave it the name because it struck us as extraordinarily like the Austrian Tyrol, where—well, of which we had happy memories, Doctor Dollar."

His blue eyes winced as they flew through the open French window, up the next precipice of bricks and mortar, to the beetling sky-line of other roofs, all a little softened in the faint haze of approaching heat. It cost him a palpable effort to bring them back to the little dark consulting-room, with its cool slabs of aged oak and the summer fernery that hid the hearth.

"It's good of you to let me take my time, doctor, but yours is too valuable to waste. All I meant was to give you an idea of our surroundings, as I know they are held to count in such cases. We are embedded in pines and firs. Some people find trees depressing, but after India they were just what we wanted, and even now my wife won't let me cut down one of them. Yet depression is no name for her state of mind; it's nearer melancholy madness, and latterly she has become subject to—to delusions—which are influencing her whole character and actions in the most alarming way. We are finding it difficult, for the first time in our lives, to keep servants; even her own nephew, who has come to live with us, only stands it for my sake, poor boy! As for my nerves—well, thank God I used to think I hadn't got any when I was in the service; but it's a little hard to be—to be as we are—at our time of life!" His hot face flamed. "What am I saying? It's a thousand times harder on *her*! She had been looking forward to these days for years."

Dollar wanted to wring one of the great brown, restless hands. Might he ask the nature of the delusions?

The General cried: "I'd give ten years of my life if I could tell you!"

"You can tell me what form they take?"

"I must, of course; it is what I came for, after all," the General muttered. He raised his head and his voice together.

"Well, for one thing she's got herself a ferocious bulldog and a revolver."

Dollar did not move a doctor's muscle. "I suppose there must be a dog in the country, especially where there are no children. And if you must have a dog, you can't do better than a bulldog. Is there any reason for the revolver? Some people think it another necessity of the country."

"It isn't with us—much less as she carries it."

"Ladies in India get in the habit, don't they?"

"She never did. And now——"

"Yes, General? Has she it always by her?"

"Night and day, on a curb bracelet locked to her wrist!"

This time there were no professional pretenses. "I don't wonder you have trouble with your servants," said Dollar, with as much sympathy as he liked to show.

"You mayn't see it when you come down, doctor, as I am going to entreat you to do. She has her sleeves cut on purpose, and it is the smallest you can buy. But I know it's always there—and always loaded."

Dollar played a while with a queer plain steel ruler, out of keeping with his other possessions, though it too had its history. It stood on end before he let it alone and looked up.

"General Dysone, there must be some sort of reason or foundation for all this. Has anything alarming happened since you have been at—Valsugana?"

"Nothing that firearms could prevent"

"Do you mind telling me what it is that has happened?"

"We had a tragedy in the winter—a suicide on the place."

"Ah!"

"Her gardener hanged himself. Hers, I say, because the garden is my wife's affair. I only paid the poor fellow his wages."

"Well, come, General, that was enough to depress anybody——"

"Yet she wouldn't have even that tree cut down—nor yet come away for a change—not for as much as a night in town!"

The interruption had come with another access of grim heat and further use of the General's handkerchief. Dollar took up his steel tube of a ruler and trained it like a spy-glass on the ink, with one eye as carefully closed as if the truth lay at the bottom of the blue-black well.

"Was there any rhyme or reason for the suicide?"

"One was suggested that I would rather not repeat."

The closed eye opened to find the blue pair fallen. "I think it might help, General. Mrs. Dysone is evidently a woman of strong character, and anything———"

"She is, God knows!" cried the miserable man. "Everybody knows it now—her servants especially—though nobody used to treat them better. Why, in India—but we'll let it go at that, if you don't mind. I have provided for the widow."

Dollar bowed over his bit of steel tubing, but this time put it down so hastily that it rolled off the table. General Dysone was towering over him with shaking hand outstretched.

"I can't say any more," he croaked. "You must come down and see her for yourself; then you could do the talking—and I shouldn't feel such a damned cur! By God, sir, it's awful, talking about one's own wife like this, even for her own good! It's worse than I thought it would be. I know it's different to a doctor—but—but you're an old soldierman as well, aren't you? Didn't I hear you were in the war?"

"I was."

"Well, then," cried the General, and his blue eyes lit up with simple cunning, "that's where we met! We've run up against each other again, and I've asked you down for this next week-end! Can you manage it? Are you free? I'll write you a check for your own fee this minute, if you like—there must be nothing of that kind down there. You don't mind being Captain Dollar again, if that was it, to my wife?"

His pathetic eagerness, his sensitive loyalty—even his sudden and solicitous zest in the pious fraud proposed—made between them an irresistible appeal. Dollar had to think; the rooms up-stairs were not empty; but none enshrined a more interesting case than this sounded. On the other hand, he had to be on his guard against a weakness for mere human interest as apart from the esoteric principles of his practise. People might call him an empiric—empiric he was proud to be, but it was and must remain empiricism in one definite direction only. Psychical research was not for him—and the Dysone story had a psychic flavor.

In the end he said quite bluntly:

"I hope you don't suggest a ghost behind all this, General?"

"I? Lord, no! I don't believe in 'em," cried the warrior, with a nervous laugh.

"Does any member of your household?"

"Not—now."

"*Not* now?"

"No. I think I am right in saying that." But something was worrying him. "Perhaps it is also right," he continued, with the engaging candor of an overthrown reserve, "and only fair—since I take it you are coming—to tell you that there was a fellow with us who thought he saw things. But it was all the most utter moonshine. He saw brown devils in flowing robes, but what he'd taken before he saw them I can't tell you! He didn't stay with me long enough for us to get to know each other. But he wasn't just a servant, and it was before the poor gardener's affair. Like so many old soldiers on the shelf, Doctor Dollar, I am writing a book, and I run a secretary of sorts; now it's Jim Paley, a nephew of ours; and thank God he has more sense."

"Yet even he gets depressed?"

"He has had cause. If our own kith and kin behaved like one possessed——" He stopped himself yet again; this time his hand found Dollar's with a vibrant grip. "You will come, won't you? I can meet any train on Saturday, or any other day that suits you better. I—for her own sake, doctor—I sometimes feel it might be better if she went away for a time. But you will come and see her for yourself?"

Before he left it was a promise; a harder heart than John Dollar's would have ended by making it, and putting the new case before all others when the Saturday came. But it was not only his prospective patient whom the crime doctor was now really anxious to see; he felt fascinated in advance by the scene and every person of an indubitable drama, of which at least one tragic act was already over.

There was no question of meeting him at any station; the wealthy mother of a still recent patient had insisted on presenting Doctor Dollar with a fifteen-horse-power

Talboys, which he had eventually accepted, and even chosen for himself (with certain expert assistance), as an incalculable contribution to the Cause. Already the car had vastly enlarged his theater of work; and on every errand his heart was lightened and his faith fortified by the wonderful case of the young chauffeur who sat so upright at the wheel beside him. In the beginning he had slouched there like the worst of his kind; it was neither precept nor reprimand which had straightened his back and his look and all about him. He was what John Dollar had always wanted—the unconscious patient whose history none knew—who himself little dreamed that it was all known to the man who treated him almost like a brother.

The boy had been in prison for dishonesty; he was being sedulously trusted, and so taught to trust himself. He had come in March, a sulky and suspicious clod; and now in June he could talk cricket and sixpenny editions from the Hounslow tram-lines to the wide white gate opening into a drive through a Berkshire wood, with a house lurking behind it in a mask of ivy, out of the sun.

But in the drive General Dysone stepped back into the doctor's life, and, on being directed to the stables, he who had filled it for the last hour drove out of it for the next twenty-four.

"I wanted you to hear something at once from me," his host whispered under the whispering trees, "lest it should be mentioned and take you aback before the others. We've had another little tragedy—not a horror like the last—yet in one way almost worse. My wife shot her own dog dead last night!"

Dollar put a curb upon his parting lips.

"*In* the night?" he stood still to ask.

"Well, between eleven and twelve."

"In her own room, or where?"

"Out-of-doors. Don't ask me how it happened; nobody seems to know, and don't *you* know anything if she speaks of it herself."

His fine face was streaming with perspiration; yet he seemed to have been waiting quietly under the trees, he was not short of breath, and he a big elderly man. Dollar asked no questions at all; they dropped the subject there in the drive. Though the sun was up somewhere out of sight, it was already late in the long June afternoon, and the guest was taken straight to his room.

It was a corner room with one ivy-darkened casement overlooking a shadowy lawn, the other facing a forest of firs and chestnuts on which it was harder to look without an instinctive qualm. But the General seemed to have forgot his tragedies, and for the moment his blue eyes almost brightened the somber scene on which they dwelt with involuntary pride.

"Now don't you see where Tyrol comes in?" said he. "Put a mountain behind those trees—and there *was* one the very first time we saw the house! It was only a thunder-cloud, but for all the world it might have been the Dolomites. And it took us back ... we had no other clouds then!"

Dollar found himself alone; found his things laid out and his shirt studded, and a cozy on the brass hot-water can, with as much satisfaction as though he had never stayed in a country house before. Could there be so very much amiss in a household where they knew just what to do for one, and just what to leave undone?

And it was the same with all the other creature comforts; they meant good servants, however short their service; and good servants do not often mean the mistress or the hostess whom Dollar had come prepared to meet. He dressed in pleasurable doubt and enhanced excitement—and those were his happiest moments at Valsugana.

Mrs. Dysone was a middle-aged woman who looked almost old, whereas the General was elderly with all the appearance of early middle age. The contrast was even more complete in more invidious particulars; but Dollar took little heed of the poor lady's face, as a lady's face. Her skin and eyes were enough for him; both were brown, with that almost ultra-Indian tinge of so many Anglo-Indians. He was sensible at once of an Oriental impenetrability.

With her conversation he could not quarrel; what there was of it was crisp, unstudied, understanding. And the little dinner did her the kind of credit for which he was now prepared; but she only once took charge of the talk, and that was rather sharply to change a subject into which she had been the first to enter.

How it had cropped up, Dollar could never think, especially as his former profession and rank duly obtained throughout his visit. He had even warned his chauffeur that he was not the doctor there; it could not have been he himself who started it, but somebody did, as somebody always does when there is one topic to avoid. It was probably the nice young nephew who made the first well-meaning remark upon the general want of originality, with reference to something or other under criticism at the moment; but it was neither he nor Dollar who laid it down that monkeys were the most arrant imitators in nature—except criminals; and it certainly was the General who said that nothing would surprise him less than if another fellow went and hanged himself in their wood. Then it was that Mrs. Dysone put her foot down—and Dollar never forgot her look.

Almost for the first time it made him think of her revolver. It was out of sight; and full as her long sleeves were, it was difficult to believe that one of them could conceal the smallest firearm made; but a tiny gold padlock did dangle when she raised her glass of water; and at the end of dinner there was a second little scene, this time without words, which went far to dispel any doubt arising in his mind.

He was holding the door open for Mrs. Dysone, and she stood a moment on the threshold, peering into the far corners of the room. He saw what it was she had forgot— saw it come back to her as she turned away, with another look worth remembering.

Either the General missed that, or the anxieties of the husband were now deliberately sunk in the duties of the host. He had got up some Jubilee port in the doctor's honor; they sat over it together till it was nearly time for bed. Dollar took little, but the other grew a shade more rubicund, and it was good to hear him chat without restraint or an apparent care. Yet it was strange as well; again he drifted into criminology, and his own after-dinner defect of sensibility only made his hearer the more uncomfortable.

Of course, he felt, it was partly out of compliment to himself as crime doctor; but the ugly subject had evidently an unhealthy fascination of its own for the fine full-blooded man. Not that it seemed an inveterate foible; the expert observer thought it rather the reflex attraction of the strongest possible horror and repulsion, and took it the more seriously on that account. Of two evils it seemed to him the less to allow himself to be pumped on professional generalities. It was distinctly better than encouraging the General to ransack his long experience for memories of decent people who had done dreadful deeds. Best of all to assure him that even those unfortunates might have outlived their infamy under the scientific treatment of a more enlightened day.

If they must talk crime, let it be the Cure of Crime! So the doctor had his heart-felt say; and the General listened even more terribly than he had talked; asking questions in whispers, and waiting breathless for the considered reply. It was the last of these that took most answering.

"And which, doctor, for God's sake, which would you have most hope of curing: a man or a woman?"

But Dollar would only say: "I shouldn't despair of *anybody*, who had done *anything*, if there was still an intelligence to work upon; but the more of that the better."

And the General said hardly another word, except "God bless you!" outside the spare-room door. His wife had been seen no more.

But Dollar saw her in every corner of his delightful quarters; and the acute contrast that might have unsettled an innocent mind had the opposite effect on his. There were electric lamps in all the right places; there were books and biscuits, a glass of milk, even a miniature decanter and a bottle of Schweppes. He sighed as he wound his watch and placed it in the little stand on the table beside the bed; but he was only wondering exactly what he was going to discover before he wound it up again.

Outside one open window the merry crickets were playing castanets in those dreadful trees. It was the other blind that he drew up; and on the lawn the dying and reviving glow of a cigarette gave glimpses of a white shirt-front, a black satin tie, the drooping brim of a Panama hat. It was the nice young nephew, who had retreated before the Jubilee port. And Dollar was still wondering on what pretext he could go down and join him, when his knock came at the door.

"Only to see if you'd everything you want," explained young Paley, ingenuously disingenuous; and shut the door behind him before the invitation to enter was out of the doctor's mouth. But he shut it very softly, trod like a burglar, and excused himself with bated breath: "You are the first person who has stayed with us since I've been here, Captain Dollar!" And his wry young smile was as sad as anything in the sad house.

"You amaze me!" cried Dollar. Indeed, it was the flank attack of a new kind of amazement. "I should have thought—" and his glance made a lightning tour of the luxurious room.

"I know," said Paley, nodding. "I think they must have laid themselves out for visitors at the start. But none come now. I wish they did! It's a house that wants them."

"You are rather a small party, aren't you?"

"We are rather a grim party! And yet my old uncle is absolutely the finest man I ever struck."

"I don't wonder that you admire him."

"You don't know what he is, Captain Dollar. He got the V.C. when he was my age in Burmah, but he deserves one for almost every day of his ordinary home life."

Dollar made no remark; the young fellow offered him a cigarette, and was encouraged to light another himself. He required no encouragement to talk.

"The funny thing is that he's not really my uncle. I'm *her* nephew; and she's a wonderful woman, too, in her way. She runs the whole place like a book; she's thrown away here. But—I can't help saying it—I should like her better if I didn't love him!"

"Talking of books," said Dollar, "the General told me he was writing one, and that you were helping him?"

"He didn't tell you what it was about?"

"No."

"Then I mustn't. I wish I could. It's to be the last word on a certain subject, but he won't have it spoken about. That's one reason why it's getting on his nerves."

"*Is* it his book?"

"It and everything. Doesn't he remind you of a man sitting on a powder-barrel? If he weren't what he is, there'd be an explosion every day. And there never is one—no matter what happens!"

Dollar watched the pale youth swallowing his smoke.

"Do they often talk about crime?"

"Always! They can't keep off it. And Aunt Essie always changes the subject as though she hadn't been every bit as bad as uncle. Of course they've had a good lot to make them morbid. I suppose you heard about poor Dingle, the last gardener?"

"Only just"

"He was the last man you would ever have suspected of such a thing. It was in those trees just outside." The crickets made extra merry as he paused. "They didn't find him for a day and a night!"

"Look here! I'm not going to let you talk about it," said Dollar. But the good-humored rebuff cost him an effort. He wanted to hear all about the suicide, but not from this worn lad with an old man's smile. He knew and liked the type too well.

"I'm sorry, Captain Dollar." Jim Paley looked sorry. "Yet, it's all very well! I don't suppose the General told you what happened last night?"

"Well, yes, he did, but without going into any particulars."

And now the doctor made no secret of his curiosity; this was a matter on which he could not afford to forego enlightenment. Nor was it like raking up an old horror; it would do the boy more good than harm to speak of this last affair.

"I can't tell you much about it myself," said he. "I was wondering if I could, just now on the lawn. That's where it happened, you know."

"I didn't know."

"Well, it was, and the funny thing is that I was there at the time. I used to go out with the dog for a cigarette when they turned in; last night I was foolish enough to fall asleep in a chair on the lawn. I had been playing tennis all the afternoon, and had a long bike-ride both ways. Well, all I know is that I woke up thinking I'd been shot; and there was my aunt with a revolver she insists on carrying—and poor Muggins as dead as a door-nail."

"Did she say it was an accident?"

"She behaved as if it had been; she was all over the poor dead brute."

"Rather a savage dog, wasn't it?"

"I never thought so. But the General had no use for him—and no wonder! Did he tell you he had bitten him in the shoulder?"

"No."

"Well, he did, only the other day. But that's the old General all over. He never told me till the dog was dead. I shouldn't be surprised if——"

"Yes?"

"——if my aunt hadn't been in it somehow. Poor old Muggins was such a bone between them!"

"You don't suppose he'd ended by turning on her?"

"Hardly. He was like a kitten with her, poor brute!"

Another cigarette was lighted; more inhaling went on unchecked.

"Was Mrs. Dysone by herself out there—but for you?"

"Well—yes."

"Does that mean she wasn't?"

"Upon my word, I don't know!" said young Paley, frankly. "It sounds most awful rot, but just for a moment I thought I saw somebody in a sort of surplice affair. But I can only swear to Aunt Essie, and she was in her dressing-gown, and it wasn't white."

Dollar did not go to bed at all. He sat first at one window, watching the black trees turn blue, and eventually a variety of sunny greens; then at the other, staring down at the pretty scene of a deed ugly in itself, but uglier in the peculiar quality of its mystery.

A dog; only a dog, this time; but the woman's own dog! There were two new sods on the place where he supposed it had lain withering....

But who or what was it that these young men had seen—the one the General had told him about, and this obviously truthful lad whom he himself had questioned? "Brown devils in flowing robes" was perhaps only the old soldier's picturesque phrase; they might have turned brown in his Indian mind; but what of Jim Paley's "somebody in a sort of surplice affair"? Was that "body" brown as well?

In the wood of worse omen the gay little birds tuned up to deaf ears at the open window. And a cynical soloist went so far as to start saying, "Pretty, pretty, pretty, pretty!" in a liquid contralto. But a little sharp shot, fired two nights and a day before, was the only sound to get across the spare-room window-sill....

The bathroom was next door; in that physically admirable house there was boiling hot water at six o'clock in the morning; the servants made tea when they heard it running; and the garden before breakfast was almost a delight. It might have been an Eden ... it *was* ... with the serpent still in the grass!

Blinds went up like eyelids under bushy brows of ivy. The grass remained gray with dew; there was not enough sun anywhere, though the whole sky beamed. Dollar wandered indoors the way the General had taken him the day before. It was the way through his library. Libraries are always interesting; a man's bookcase is sometimes more interesting than the man himself, sometimes the one existing portrait of his mind. Dollar spent the best part of an absorbing hour without taking a single volume from its place. But this was partly because those he would have dipped into were under glass and lock and key. And partly it was due to more accessible distractions crowning that very piece of ostensible antiquity which contained the books, and of which the top drawer drew out into the General's desk.

The distractions were a peculiarly repulsive gilded idol, squatting with its tongue out, as if at the amateur author, and a heathen sword on the wall behind it. Nothing more; but Dollar also had served in India in his day, and his natural interest was whetted by a certain smattering of lore. He was still standing on a newspaper and a chair when a voice hailed him in no hospitable tone.

"Really, Captain Dollar! I should have asked the servants for a ladder while I was about it!"

Of course it was Mrs. Dysone, and she was not even pretending to look pleased. He jumped down with an apology which softened not a line of her sallow face and bony figure.

"It was an outrage," he owned. "But I did stand on a paper to save the chair. I say, though, I never noticed it was this week's *Field*."

Really horrified at his own behavior, he did his best to smooth and wipe away his footmarks on the wrapper of the paper. But those subtle eyes, like blots of ink on old parchment, were no longer trained on the offender, who missed yet another look that might have helped him.

"My husband's study is rather holy ground," was the lady's last word. "I only came in myself because I thought he was here."

Mercifully, days do not always go on as badly as they begin; more strangely, this one developed into the dullest and most conventional of country-house Sundays.

General Dysone was himself not only dull, but even a little stiff, as became a good Briton who had said too much to too great a stranger overnight. His natural courtesy had become conspicuous; he played punctilious host all day; and Dollar was allowed to feel that, if he had come down as a doctor, he was staying on as an ordinary guest, and in a house where guests were expected to observe the Sabbath. So they all marched off together to the village church, where the General trumpeted the tune in his own octave, read the lessons, and kept waking up during the sermon. There were the regulation amenities with other devout gentry of the neighborhood; there was the national Sunday sirloin at the midday meal, and no more untoward topics to make the host's forehead glisten or the hostess gleam and lower. In the afternoon the whole party inspected every animal and vegetable on the premises; and after tea the visitor's car came round.

Originally there had been much talk of his staying till the Monday; the General went through the form of pressing him once more, but was not backed up by his wife, who had shadowed them suspiciously all day. Nor did he comment on this by so much as a sidelong glance at Dollar, or contrive to get another word with him alone. And the crime doctor, instead of making any excuse to remain and penetrate these new mysteries, showed a sensitive alacrity to leave.

Of the nephew, who looked terribly depressed at his departure, he had seen something more, and had even asked two private favors. One, that he would keep out of that haunted garden for the next few nights, and try going to bed earlier; the other an odd request for an almost middle-aged man about town, but rather flattering to the young fellow. It was for the loan of his Panama, so that Dollar's hatter might see if he could not get him as good a one. Paley's was the kind that might be carried up a sleeve, like the modern handkerchief; he explained that the old General had given it him.

Dollar tried it on almost as soon as the car was out of sight of Valsugana—while his young chauffeur was still wondering what he had done to make the governor sit behind. It was funny of him, just when a chap might have been telling him a thing or two that he had heard down there at the coachman's place. But it was all the more interesting when they got back to town at seven in the evening, and he was ordered to fill up with petrol and be back at nine, to make the same trip over again.

"I needn't ask you," the doctor added, "to hold your tongue about anything you may have heard at General Dysone's. I know you will, Albert."

And almost by lighting-up time they were shoulder to shoulder on the road once more.

But at Valsugana it was another dark night, and none too easy to find one's way about the place on the strength of a midsummer day's acquaintance. And for the first time Dollar was glad the dog of the house was dead, as he finished a circuitous approach by stealing through the farther wood, toward the jagged lumps of light in the ivy-strangled bedroom windows; already everything was dark down-stairs.

Here were the pale new sods; they could just be seen, though his feet first felt their inequalities. His cigarette was the one pin-prick of light in all the garden, though each draw brought the buff brim of Jim Paley's Panama within an inch of his eyes, its fine texture like coarse matting at the range. And the chair in which Jim Paley had sat smoking this time last night, and dozing the night before when the shot disturbed him, was just where he expected his shins to find it; the wickers squeaked as John Dollar took his place.

Less need now not to make a sound; but he made no more than he could help, for the night was still and sultry, without any of the garden noises of a night ago. It was as though nature had stopped her orchestra in disgust at the plot and counterplot brewing on her darkened stage. The cigarette-end was thrown away; it might have been a stone that fell upon the grass, and Dollar could almost hear it sizzling in the dew. His aural nerves were tuned to the last pitch of sensitive acknowledgment; a fly on the drooping Panama-brim would not have failed to "scratch the brain's coat of curd." ... How much less the swift and furtive footfall that came kissing the wet lawn at last!

It was more than a footfall; there was a following swish of some long garment trailing through the wet. It all came near; it all stopped dead. Dollar had nodded heavily as if in sleep; had jerked his head up higher; seemed to be dropping off again in greater comfort.

The footfalls and the swish came on like thunder now. But now his eyelids were only drooping like the brim above them; in the broad light of their abnormal perceptivity, it was as if his own eyes threw a dreadful halo round the figure they beheld. It was a swaddled figure, creeping into monstrosity, crouching early for its spring. It had draped arms extended, with some cloth or band that looped and tightened at each stride: on the rounded shoulders bobbed the craning head and darkened face of General Dysone.

In his last stride he swerved, as if to get as much behind the chair as its position under the tree permitted. The cloth clapped as it came taut over Dollar's head, but was not actually round his neck when he ducked and turned, and hit out and up with all his might. He felt the rasp of a fifteen-hours' beard, heard the click of teeth; the lawn quaked, and white robes settled upon a senseless heap, as the plumage on a murdered pigeon.

Dollar knelt over him and felt his pulse, held an electric lamp to eyes that opened, and quickly something else to the dilated nostrils.

"O Jim!" shuddered a voice close at hand. It was shrill yet broken, a cry of horror, but like no voice he knew.

He jumped up to face the General's wife.

"It's not Jim, Mrs. Dysone. It's I—Dollar. He'll soon be all right!"

"Captain—Dollar?"

"No—doctor, nowadays—he called me down as one himself. And now I've come back on my own responsibility, and—put him under chloroform; but I haven't given him much; for God's sake let us speak plainly while we can!"

She was on her knees, proving his words without uttering one. Still kneeling speechless, she leaned back while he continued: "You know what he is as well as I do, Mrs. Dysone; you may thank God a doctor has found him out before the police! Monomania is not their business—but neither are you the one to cope with it. You have shielded your husband as only a woman will shield a man; now you must let him come to me."

195

His confidence was taking some effect; but she ignored the hands that would have helped her to her feet; and her own were locked in front of her, but not in supplication.

"And what can any of you do for him," she cried fiercely—"except take him away from me?"

"I will only answer for myself. I would control him as you can not, and I would teach him to control himself if man under God can do it. I am a criminal alienist, Mrs. Dysone, as your husband knew before he came to consult me on elaborate pretenses into which we needn't go. He trusted me enough to ask me down here; in my opinion, he was feeling his way to greater trust, in the teeth of his terrible obsession, but last night he said more than he meant to say, so to-day he wouldn't say a word. I only guessed his secret this morning—when you guessed I had! It would be safe with me against the world. But how can I take the responsibility of keeping it if he remains at large as he is now?"

"You can not," said Mrs. Dysone. "I am the only one."

Her tone was dreamy and yet hard and fatalistic; the arms in the wide dressing-gown sleeves were still tightly locked. Something brought Dollar down again beside the senseless man, bending over him in keen alarm.

"He'll be himself again directly—quite himself, I shouldn't wonder! He may have forgot what has happened; he mustn't find me here to remind him. Something he will have to know, and you are the one to break it to him, and then to persuade him to come to me. But you won't find that so easy, Mrs. Dysone, if he sees how I tricked him. He had much better think it *was* your nephew. My motor's in the lane behind these trees; let him think I never went away at all, that we connived and I am holding myself there at your disposal. It would be true—wouldn't it—after this? I'll wait night and day until I know!"

"Doctor Dollar," said Mrs. Dysone, when she had risen without aid and set him to the trees, "you may or may not know the worst about my poor husband, but you shall know it now about me. I wish you to take this—and keep it! You have had two escapes to-night."

She bared the wrist from which the smallest of revolvers dangled; he felt it in the darkness—and left it dangling.

"I heard you had one. He told me. And I thought you carried it for your own protection!" cried Dollar, seeing into the woman at last.

"No. It was not for that"—and he knew that she was smiling through her tears. "I did save his life—when my poor dog saved Jim's—but I carried this to save the secret I am going to trust to you!"

Dollar would only take her hand. "You wouldn't have shot me, or any man," he assured her. "But," he added to himself among the trees, "what a fool I was to forget that *they* never killed women!"

It turned almost cold beside the motor in the lane; the doctor gave his boy a little brandy, and together they tramped up and down, talking sport and fiction by the small hour together. The stars slipped out of the sky, the birds began, and the same cynic shouted "Pretty, pretty, pretty!" at the top of its strong contralto. At long last there came that other sound for which Dollar had never ceased listening. And he turned back into the haunted wood with Jim Paley.

The poor nephew—still stunned calm—was as painfully articulate as a young bereaved husband. He spoke of General Dysone as of a man already dead, in the gentlest of past tenses. He was dead enough to the boy. There had been an appalling confession—made as coolly, it appeared, as Paley repeated it.

"He thought *I* knocked him down, and I had to let him think so! Aunt Essie insisted; she *is* a wonder, after all! It made him tell me things I simply can't believe.... Yet he showed me a rope just like it—meant for me!"

"Do you mean just like the one that—hanged the gardener?"

"Yes. *He* did it, so he swears ... *afterward*. He'll tell you himself—he wants to tell you. He says he first ... I can't put my tongue to it!" The lapse into the present tense had made him human.

"Like the Thugs?"

"Yes—like that sect of fiendish fanatics who went about strangling everybody they met! *They* were what his book was about. How did you know?"

"That's Bhowanee, their goddess, on top of his bureau, and he has Sleeman and all the other awful literature locked up underneath. As a study for a life of sudden idleness, in the depths of the country, it was enough to bring on temporary insanity. And the strong man gone wrong goes and does what the rest of us only get on our nerves!"

Dollar felt his biceps clutched and clawed, and the two stood still under more irony in a gay contralto.

"Temporary, did you say? Only *temporary?*" the boy was faltering.

"I hope so, honestly. You see, it was just on that one point ... and even there ... I believe he *did* want his wife out of the way, and for her own sake, too!" said Dollar, with a sympathetic tremor of his own.

"But do you know what he's saying? He means to tell the whole world now, and let them hang him, and serve him right—he says! And he's as sane as we are now—only he might have been through a Turkish bath!"

"More signs!" cried Dollar, looking up at the brightening sky. "But we won't allow that. It would undo nothing and he has made all the reparation.

" ... Come, Paley! I want to take him back with me in the car. It's broad daylight."

VII

THE DOCTOR'S ASSISTANT

The doctor was coping with his Sunday meal when the telephone went off in the next room. On his ears the imperious summons never fell without a thrill; in his sight, the tulip-shaped receiver became a live thing trumpeting for help; and he would answer the call himself, at any hour of the day or night. It was necessary at night, with the Bartons asleep in the basement like a family in a vault, but it was just the same when they were all on duty, as at the present moment. Back went the Cromwellian chair, at the head of the bare and solitary trestle table. An excited personage, who might have been just outside the window, was expeditiously appeased in monosyllables. And Dollar returned with an appetite to what had been set before him.

"Send Bobby round to the garage, Barton, to order the car at once. He can tell Albert I shall be ready as soon as he is, but to take his headlights and fill up with petrol." This was repeated with paternal severity in the wings. "Now, Barton, my little red road-book, and see if you can find Pax Monktons in the wilds of Surrey. It can't be more than a hamlet. Try the Cobham country if it's not in the index."

This took longer—took a survey map and two pairs of eyes before Pax Monktons Chase was discovered in microscopic print, and the light green peppered with dots signifying timber three hundred feet above sea-level.

"Never heard of it in my life before," said Dollar, as he laced brown shoes before his coffee. "Or of the man either, or his double-barreled name for that matter. You might see if there's a Dale-Bulmer in *Who's Who*."

But again Barton was unsuccessful; and here his services ended, though through no fault of his own, or failure of unselfish zeal for one of those more than probable adventures which made him hate the chauffeur who was always in them, and curse the duties that kept other people out.

"Will you take your flask, sir?"

"Lord, no! I'm not going to the North Pole."

"Or your—or one of those revolvers, sir?"

"What on earth for? Besides, they're not mine; they ought to be in the Black Museum at Scotland Yard." The nucleus of a branch exhibition was forming itself in Welbeck Street. "Don't you give way to nerves, Barton! I'm only going down to see a man who seems anxious to see me, but I shouldn't be going to him if we had anybody up-stairs. You three make an afternoon of it somewhere; never mind if I'm back first; go out and enjoy yourselves."

And he was off as if on a deliberate jaunt; but an involuntary chuckle in the voice over the telephone, the hint of a surprise, the possibility of a trick, made lively thinking after the doldrums of the dog-days; and the fine September afternoon seemed expressly ordered for motorists with time upon their hands. Dollar had only been thinking so when the call came through, to supply just the object which gives a run its zest, and nothing else mattered in the least. However frivolous the end and errand, the means and the meantime were so much to the good on such a day.

It was warm, yet delightfully keen at thirty miles an hour; clear as crystal within rifle-shot, and deliciously hazy in the distance; the bronze upon the trees seldom warming to a premature red, often lapsing into the liquid greens of midsummer; but all the way an autumnal smear of silver in the sunlight. Dollar divided his mind between a sensuous savoring of the heavenly country, and more or less romantic speculations on the case in store. Some people's notions of a crime doctor's functions were so much wider even than his own; ten months out of the twelve, he could not have afforded to come so far afield without a distastefully definite foreword about fees.

This afternoon he was prepared to do almost anything for next to nothing: and after twenty sedentary miles he was on his legs as often as not in the next two or three, asking his way at likely lodges, or from strolling bands of shaven yokels, all Sunday collars and cigarettes.

"Pax Monktons Chase?" at last said one who seemed to have heard the name before. "Straight as ever you can go, and the first lodge on the left. But there's no one there."

"No one there!" echoed Dollar. "Do you mean the place is empty?"

"I believe there's workmen there on week-days, but you won't find anybody now, unless the chap that's bought it's motored over."

"Isn't he living there, then?"

"Not yet; there's alterations being made; and I don't know where he does live, or anything at all about him, except that he motors over sometimes on a Sunday."

Dollar felt dashed until he remembered to appreciate one of the few possibilities for which he had not come quite prepared. There was some promise in a surprise thus early and so complete. But it made Pax Monktons Chase fall a little flat when found. It robbed the dreary lodge of all its value as an eye-opener; it made the chase itself look vast and desolate for nothing, and a noble pile of seasoned stone fling but drab turrets and ineffective battlements against a silver sky, which the sun had ceased to polish in the last tortuous mile.

It was all the pleasanter to find a ruddy, genial, bearded face, mounted on a spotted tie that went twice round a nineteen-inch neck, smiling a welcome under the entrance arch. The man introduced himself as Dale-Bulmer, bolting a mouthful made for rolling on the tongue. Dollar was much taken with the humor and simplicity of his address and bearing. A smart chauffeur waited with a plutocratic car in the sweep of the drive. And there was no third sign of life about the place.

"Awfully good of you to come," said Dale-Bulmer, with apologetic warmth. "I thought you might, from what I'd heard of you, and you seemed to jump at it when I rang you up. I haven't known anybody take so kindly to a trip since I left the bush."

"An Australian?" asked the doctor, with all a doctor's readiness to make talk; but he was more curious than ever to learn the secret of his summons.

"Yes! I come from that enlightened land, where Labor runs the show and Women have the Vote. In fact," the big man added, with the fat chuckle heard over the telephone, "that's precisely why I *have* come from Australia—as I was fool enough to say the other night at a meeting in these parts. But I seem to have jumped out of the frying-pan into the fire."

There was no sign of life

"I'm sorry to hear that," observed Dollar, with polite forbearance.

"Well, not quite into the fire, as it happens," said Dale-Bulmer, chuckling again in his noble neck. "Come inside, and you'll see." He led the way into a broad central corridor, choked with ladders and builders' tools, pipes and tubing, curtain-rods, and a stack of boards; but a model of order compared with the chaos visible through an open door at which he paused. Here were more bare joists than navigable floor, and a forest of scaffolding therefrom to the crisscrossed plaster ceiling. "Look you here!" said the man from Australia, and pointed to a heap of shavings on a remnant of the floor.

"The British workman's such a careless dog," sighed Dollar, shaking a sententious head, for a box of vestas had been spilt about the place.

"British workman be hanged!" cried the other bluntly. "The British workman's got a job here that will keep him in beer and betting-money till Christmas, and as much longer as he can spin it out. This is the little game of another sporting type—the British lady burning for the vote!"

"So that's it! But are you sure?" asked Dollar, though he wanted to ask if that was all.

"Certain. I met a flaming brace of 'em on bicycles, just outside my boundary. This is what I was to get for speaking out about them the other night."

"I don't see their literature, and I can't smell their paraffin."

"It's in that bottle on the mantelpiece. Something must have scared them at the last moment—all but one sportswoman."

"What about her?"

"I've got her," said Dale-Bulmer, with sepulchral excitement.

"Got her prisoner?"

"I should hope so! Why, I caught her on the very point of setting fire to that very heap of shavings—and me without a hose-pipe in the house! Those are her matches on the floor; *she* wasn't going to turn tail till she'd done her job—and didn't till I nearly trod on it! You could hardly expect me to bow her out of the front door after that!"

Dollar could only stare into the jovial face wreathed in rubicund grins, but no longer free from a certain serio-comic compunction and concern.

"But, my dear sir——"

"Don't pitch into me!" pleaded Dale-Bulmer, pathetically. "I had to do something; if I hadn't thought of you, and one or two things I've heard about you, doctor, I should only have telephoned to the police; and what's the good of putting these young women in the jug, to be poured out again within a week? I heard you ran a nursing-home for criminals, worth all the prisons in the world."

"But I don't run people into it," said the doctor; "they've got to come in of their own free will. What have you done with this young woman?"

"I? Nothing; it's her own doing entirely. She chose her cover—I only turned the key."

"You've locked her up in some room?"

"Yes—more or less—rather more."

And Dale-Bulmer laughed a rather nervous, guilty laugh.

"Up-stairs somewhere?"

"Yes—look you here! She was picking up those matches when I spotted her from this door, and out she streaked through that one over there. Come and have a look at her line of country, doctor."

It led into an anteroom or inner hall, or the well of some staircase still to come, with a lashed ladder towering in its midst, but not quite reaching a skeleton landing of yawning joists. Dale-Bulmer gazed aloft, wagging a horizontal beard.

"Surely she didn't go up there?" said Dollar.

"Like a lamplighter, doctor! I went the way we'll both go now, if it's all the same to you."

A fine forked staircase bore them from the lower corridor to its counterpart above. And here the leader trod gently, a finger laid across his lips.

"That's the room," he whispered, pointing to a shut door in a side passage. "I—I almost think I'll leave her to you, doctor. It's not locked—not the door."

"I thought she was your prisoner?"

"Yes—but you'll see where she's hidden herself. I did turn *that* key, doctor, but that's all I did. Still, I think I'd rather you let her out."

There was nothing facetious in his droll air of guilt; he seemed really rather ashamed of his impetuous measures, as if long in doubt as to their gallantry, and abashed by the unspoken criticisms of the man whom he had brought so far afield on the spur of a flustering moment. But the truth was that Dollar did not blame him in the least, as he turned the handle softly, and heard a pusillanimous step retreating down the corridor.

It was a light and lofty room, with a broad bay-window overlooking the park; and in the bay a window-seat forming a coffer, which had been broken open from within; and just clear of the splinters, her hands raised to her disheveled hair, hat awry and country clothes begrimed, a young woman risen like Aphrodite from the foam. She had been gazing out as she put herself to rights; but at the opening of the door she turned with a light disdain, and the pair of them stood rooted to the floor.

"Lady—Vera!" he could only gasp.

She made him an abrupt little bow; then her head went back to the truculent angle necessitated by a jelly-bag hat worn almost as a mask; and her eyes hung under the brim like great blue rain-drops, grim and gleaming, but with little of his blank amazement, and nothing of the shame that shook his soul.

"No wonder you would never see me!" he muttered more to himself than to her. "Not a word even when I wrote—and I wondered what I'd done! I thought of heaps of things—but I never thought of this!"

She shook her head as abruptly as she had bowed; the blue rain-drops looked frozen where they hung, but the firm lips parted impulsively. Instinct prepared him for something inconceivable. But her self-restraint was a lesson and a reproof; and, in laying it to heart and listening to what she did say he for the moment ceased from wondering what it was that she had just kept back—what charge she had deferred against him.

"Tell me one thing, Doctor Dollar." Her voice was all that it had been in other emergencies, only colder by some degrees. "Have you been following me, or is this pure chance?"

"Not chance—pure Fate!"

"Did you dog me down here, or did you not?"

"Not consciously. Do I look as if I had?"

"You look as if you'd seen a ghost," she told him, with a sudden twinkle of the big blue drops.

"So I have!" he cried in passionate earnest. "I've seen the ghost of everything I held most——"

"Thank you," she said quietly, when he had checked himself on her model. "I know what you must think—what you really have a special right to think—after two years ago. Do be generous and don't say it! This isn't altogether fun for me, you know, much less after being buried alive for hours!" She just turned her head toward the broken window-seat, and his eyes devoured the light upon her profile. "What's going to happen to me? Is my natural enemy a friend of yours? Has he sent for the police?"

"No—for me instead."

"Did he know who it was at sight?"

"He didn't, and he doesn't, and he never shall unless you tell him!" exclaimed Dollar vehemently. "O Vera, when I was longing to see you, to warn you against your enemies, that you should go the way to put yourself more than ever in their power!"

A glitter under the tilted hat had unconsciously rebuked an unconscious liberty; yet once this man had begged this woman to marry him, and once she had practically said she would but for the burden on her soul. Ceremony, at least, they had foregone of old. Was it merely her new lease of error that had come between them of late months? He was

211

beginning to ask himself the question when she broke in with one of her own:

"What enemies do you mean, Doctor Dollar?"

"We are not to speak of two years ago."

"Croucher!" She shuddered almost like a law-abiding lady. "I haven't heard of him since that night in the train."

"I said you wouldn't But I also said, if you remember, that Croucher was only deadly as a tool. Well, he has fallen into the deadliest hands I know—that's all."

It was not, and Lady Vera knew that it was not. The angle of her hat was all amicable attention now, and her eyes shone clear of the brim, with a softer light that made her all at once incredible in her latest incarnation. Dollar's feelings flew back into his face; she read them with a smile that made him wince, by its cynical resemblance to one or two that still enriched his dreams.

"You think I'm as bad as any of them," she divined aloud.

"I think the crime of arson is worse than most crimes," he made sturdy answer, standing up to the little body with the strangest difficulty, as though he were the culprit and she the man. "It's a thing absolutely nothing on earth can possibly excuse. I think you'd have died rather than descend to it—two years ago!"

He had heard a step behind him, and lowered his voice; but Lady Vera raised hers as a burly form halted shyly on the threshold; and her tone was like none that she had taken hitherto.

"Two years ago," she declaimed, "women had not been treated quite so shabbily as they have been since. Then this miserable Government—"

"Look you here!" blustered Dale-Bulmer, striding out of his shyness into the center of the stage.

"Two years ago," she reiterated for his benefit, "it wasn't war to the handle of the knife! Now it would be fire and sword, if we were any good with the sword; as we are not, it's simply fire!"

"You really think you can burn your way to political power?" cried the man of extremes, with ungovernable indignation.

"Political existence is all we ask."

"As a first instalment! I know you! I come from a country where you started just like that!"

"As you told your audience the other night, if you are Mr. Dale-Bulmer," said Lady Vera, with an explosive little sigh.

"I am; and for that I'm to have a house like this burned to the ground; and you ladies think that's the way to advance your cause, to prove your value to the State! Well, I suppose you know your own business best. It's no use reasoning with you; but it really is enough to set one off, after what I caught you doing down-stairs."

"I wish to goodness you hadn't caught me," cried Lady Vera, with quite extraordinary simplicity.

But neither of them took her up; the doctor could only shake his head in professional despair, while the injured householder recovered his composure, and the little criminal looked as if she were trying not to look the mistress of the situation.

"I only came," resumed Dale-Bulmer, rather as one who had no right in the room, "to say that a run-about car has been found in the yard behind one of the empty lodges. As I fancy your friends were on bicycles, it struck me that the two-seater might perhaps be yours?"

Was it just the nature of the man to change his whole manner in a moment, or had the quality of the woman something to do with it? He seemed unconscious of the change himself—unaware that he had dropped into a tone of courteous consideration bordering almost on the apologetic. But the corners of her little mutinous mouth showed that nothing was lost upon Lady Vera.

"It sounds like mine," she confessed without indecent amusement. "But I hope you don't think, because there's room for two, that there's another of us still concealed about the premises? I came down quite by myself, in the car you have discovered. And who's to drive it back to town again, I'm sure *I* don't know!"

Dale-Bulmer glanced defiantly at Dollar, a flash-light in his eyes.

"I do," he cried. "Yourself!"

"Myself, Mr. Dale-Bulmer? In—handcuffs?"

And it was not her worst smile that was subdued in deference to the full glow of his shamefaced magnanimity.

"Don't talk nonsense!" said he gruffly. "Your car is ready waiting for you at the door."

"Not really?"

"Of course. I buried you alive, didn't I?" His eyes came from the wrecked window-seat. "Won't that meet the immediate case for martyrdom?" And he managed another twinkle after all.

It was a last amenity. He had been thanked, but without the smile which had been ready enough when it was out of place; now that she had cause to smile, the perversity of these women came out, as of course it would! Not that this one took everything quite for granted; on the contrary, she caused an explosion by offering to pay for the damage to the window-seat. The militant party would have wished him to secure ample compensation from his insurance people, she asserted, if the place *had* been burned down. "Then I might have built the kind of house I really want, instead of trying to make a silk purse out of a sow's ear!" he had retorted in his better manner, as though he had been a fool to interfere.

But it was not his best manner; it was almost as unrepresentative as the calm self-centered way in which the released prisoner spent the last minutes looking for her gloves, and, when she failed to find them, held out her bare hand with a brazen air of innocence, and no more thanks than would have become a parting guest.

Even John Dollar felt a new pang of disappointment as the two-seater shrank panting out of sight and ear-shot, beneath the bronzed timber of the disappearing drive, and Dale-Bulmer turned on his heel under the arch.

"Doesn't that take the cake?" he cried, when he had swallowed his pique with a chastened chuckle. "A real well-bred 'un—if ever there was one—playing the very devil, and carrying it off like a little angel of light! That's what did me—the way she carried it off! I wanted to give her a fatherly word, to tell her not to go on making such a wicked little fool of herself. But she simply wouldn't look the part, would she? I hadn't even the cheek to ask her name—had you?"

"No. I don't know why you let her off," said Dollar, irritably; but at the moment he hated Dale-Bulmer for extorting his common gratitude at the expense of his sacred flame.

"Why?" cried that cavalier. "Didn't you guess how I found out about her car?"

"How?"

"Reported to me by the police!"

"The police? Were there any about?"

Dollar felt as cold down the back as though his sacred flame had never flickered behind iron bars.

"Two blighters," said Dale-Bulmer. "I caught sight of 'em just after I had left you to have it out with her. That's what they had to say for themselves when I went out to let off steam; swore they were from Scotland Yard, and trumped up the two-seater when I pretended not to believe them. Nor did I till I'd run them down to the lodge and seen it for myself."

"And then?"

"I swore it belonged to a friend, of course, and sent them both to the devil."

"And—and you were man enough not to say a word about it to—to her?" It was as much as Dollar could do to keep his enthusiastic respect within bounds of discretion.

"Man enough? I wasn't going to have that sort of carrion coming in and spoiling *your* job!"

Then he perceived how he had spoilt it himself; hung his great head like an elderly elephantine schoolboy; turned his broad back with an inimitable shrug, and stood shaken to the pit with sobs of mirth. Dollar joined him with a shout that relieved them both. And they roared together until a gaunt caretaker appeared on the scene, with a face expressive of such crass bewilderment that their poor clay quaked with a second shock.

"He lives in the bowels of the house," moaned Dale-Bulmer. "He doesn't know a thing that's happened. If he did I might have to double his screw. And—and I'd much rather treble your fee!"

He was solemn once more in his remorse, but not so solemn as the doctor had become within a minute.

"I would *pay* a fee to take his place till to-morrow morning! I mean it, my dear sir. If you think you owe me any little amends, let me do this, for my own satisfaction!"

This from a Dollar at whom the other stared as though they had only just met. It was the crime doctor come at last.

"Stay here for the night, Doctor Dollar?"

"Yes—alone."

"But why, my good fellow?"

"I can hardly tell you; only let me stay, if you can trust me!"

"You know it isn't that."

"Then do let me! It isn't so much for your sake—I won't pretend it is—yet what if there should be a second attempt on the house? Then I might even earn the fee you talk about; otherwise, not a brass farthing! I wouldn't have missed the case for anything, even as it stands. And you only took my treatment out of my mouth; you did the very thing I was going to beg you to do, but not more earnestly than I beg of you now to leave me in charge here to-night."

"But not without this man of mine to look after you?"

"Especially without that man of yours! He gave me the idea—he's my own height and build—we can change places beautifully. I want him to put on my cap and coat and goggles, and to drive away in my car, so that anybody looking would think they had seen the last of me."

"But who should be looking? Surely not that little——"

"God forbid! But perhaps somebody on her side—or perhaps only somebody on her tracks. Curious about those two detectives; but the whole business bristles with curiosities, which I long to investigate in peace, unknown to the whole outside world. This is the only way it can be done; and this, my dear Mr. Dale-Bulmer, is the one and only thing that you can do for me!"

The boy with the beard gave way by inches. As long as there was a dog's chance of any further excitement, he did not see why he should be out of it, much less in his own house, and after the humdrum life he had led since Labor and the Ladies had driven him home from Australia. But the man with the stronger will seemed perfectly sincere in his further asserations that there were features in the case which he wanted to study for his own private and professional ends; that he honestly believed, they had no more to fear from their friends the enemy, but that somebody ought to remain on guard, that he was the obvious man. All this rang true enough; and but for Dollar's strange anxiety in the matter, and Dale-Bulmer's sudden discovery that he squinted, the plan might have gained earlier acceptance than it did. It was settled, however, by a timely telephone call from the Australian's furnished house at Esher, to ask if anything had happened to him, and was he never going to tear himself away from Pax Monktons Chase?

Thus it was nearly five o'clock before the crime doctor was alone at last, with certain plain quarters and plainer fare at his disposal, but with every nook and cranny of a country mansion to himself until next morning. The situation had the intrinsic charm of all lonely vigils; even if nothing was likely to come of this one, it would at least afford that continuous possibility of a thrill which becomes more thrilling than the thrill itself. And the whole business was supremely after John Dollar's heart; nothing could have been more congenial to him; and yet, though he did look forward to the night, and whatever the night might still bring forth, it was not for the night's sake that he had maneuvered to remain in the empty house. It was for the residue of daylight, and the systematic investigations it would enable him to make.

On these he started, with the precaution of a seaman marooned on a desolate island, not indubitably uninhabited, as soon as the front door shut upon Dale-Bulmer and the two chauffeurs, with the gaunt caretaker his muffled image in his own car. And these motorists were not followed out of sight or hearing, from the fading pile that looked so empty in the drooping eye of heaven. But it very soon seemed to the man within as if the whole house were a-hum with its own abysmal silence, and his lightest breath a stertorous disturbance of its ponderous peace.

He began by searching the unfurnished room in which the fire would have originated. There could be no doubt about the fell attempt so nearly made. It would have been diabolically certain of success. The scaffolding, like sticks in a gigantic grate; the draft through the joists, where the floor had been taken up; the natural flue formed by the adjoining well, so lofty that an ordinary ladder was too short to reach the landing—all these were as bellows and chimney, and the best of fuel ready laid for lighting. And here were the shavings, all nicely swept together, and the matches spilled at the last moment; as Dollar put them back into the box, his finger-tips ached for all they might have learned from that which they held—for the whole truth about the guilty hand which had let the match-box fall.

It was the whole truth, too, that he was seeking next upon his knees, in the rubble down between the joists; some fresh fact, still inconceivable as a concrete discovery, that he hoped against hope to find and to set against the facts beyond dispute. Facts could not lie, but they might exaggerate; somewhere, surely, there must be something to extenuate, something to redeem even this atrocious attempt, if only the silent walls could speak up for one who never made excuses for herself!

It was a childish instinct, a quite babyish yearning to undo what has once been done, and yet this had been the spring of that dense desire to be left behind in the house at all costs. Then he had only felt it, like a dull ache; now it became a dear and poignant conviction that there was some discovery still to make, and that he was the man to make it; that one of these walls had a word to say to him, and to him alone.

But it was none of the new bricks and mortar, wanting even their first coat of plaster; it was nothing under the lofty rafters of a quiet baronial hall where the builder had not been turned loose, nor any intruder left a trace; it was not in the round room, filled with a first instalment of the Dale-Bulmer furniture, nor yet anywhere else down-stairs, in spite of the shrill tale told by the scullery window. There the Amazons had entered, after breaking a pane like journeymen burglars. They had fled incontinently by the door. But what else had they done, and where else had they been, within those sardonically silent walls?

Had they been up-stairs before Vera Moyle ran up the ladder? Dollar returned to that speaking spot, and climbed up gingerly, in an agony of enthusiasm for her misused pluck. The gap between the top rung and the new landing was unpleasant even for him, and he was at least a foot taller than the little fool. The little fool! A pretty way to think of her, even now; but there was a worse way; and still there was a better, vaguely haunting him all the time, but almost ceasing to be vague in the room where he had found her in the flesh. He could see her there again. She had not faced him like a little fool, but a little heroine, God forgive her! Not so much as a pout about her horrible imprisonment under the window-seat! Not a moment's loss of dignity, even after that; not a moment's loss of temper. Head up, and eyes shining in the shadow of her wicked little hat!

Here, to an inch, he had caught her gazing out of that window, out and down into the chase—rolling right up to the house on this side—beating against a breakwater of a sunk fence just underneath, and dotted with leafy sail. Deer in the distance, and swallows darting across and across the window, like shuttles weaving the scene in silk, brought the picture back to good dry land. But the wide sky was still rather like a sea-sky; and it had lightened again with the approach of evening; there were silver rims to the clouds, as John Dollar tore himself from the enchanted scene.

"Now look at this one"

It was nearly dark when he returned unsteadily, with a face like a cheer—with a face that would have lighted up a tomb. In his hands he clasped a pair of innocent little gloves, that anybody might have found, and somebody traced to their beloved little owner. But that was not all. A wall had spoken, in certain handwriting hastily rubbed out, and a whole bathroom had told a yet more eloquent tale!

Hours later they were speaking still, wafting sweet music through the corridors, filling the honored room with strains of joy for the enchanted man on the broken window-seat, all in the dark at dead of night. There might have been a moon; he did not know. There might have been a stealthy advance, in very open order—a taking of cover behind trees wide apart—a joining of forces down there in the dark, that was not so dark if one was used to it. But Dollar had been for hours gazing into his own heart, and that was still so dazzlingly alight that he might not have seen anything if he had looked out; it still sang so loud that he heard nothing down-stairs until there was noise enough to wake a deeper dreamer out of actual sleep.

Even then he scarcely knew what had brought him so suddenly to feet grown numb, but not more numb than the whole outer man in the endless inner joy of that which he believed himself to have discovered along with his dear lady's gloves. Those sacred relics he still clasped in his hands, and that fond belief he was still hugging in his heart, when a louder sound pricked his undertaking to the quick. It was the sound of voices in the empty house. He tore off his shoes, limped over to the door, opened it as softly, and stood listening in a heavy horror. They were women's voices, accompanied by the scuttle of women's feet!

In an instant, but still with an instinctive stealth, he was out on the landing at the head of the stairs. And there, but only there, his fond dream ended in an awakening as terrible as any nightmare; for one woman stood on the half-landing between the two prongs of the forked staircase; all attention she stood, as if on guard; hair silvered by a shaft of moonshine through the staircase window, shoulders hunched intently, but the head itself just tilted as if in sudden alarm, and full in the moonlight the wicked unmistakable little hat of Lady Vera Moyle.

Her gloves dropped out of his hands. Did she hear them fall? She looked as if she had; he had not the heart to make sure. He had nothing like the heart to confront and shame her first—at her worst a passive party to the crime—when her guiltier companions were even then at their vile work lower down. The ladder was the thing! Then he could scare those others first, and she and he need never meet at all. Better never again than at this hideous juncture! And as for him, better death itself than such a death to such a dream!

It was a sheer stampede the man made now, back along the landing with great heavy strides, even shouting as he went to put the she-devils to flight. It was what he called them as he ran; had they not dragged an angel into this. And they heard him, and he heard them—scuttling and clucking in headlong flight.

This time they could afford to fly; their second attempt was no failure like the first. The little new landing was like a gridiron over a flickering glare from the well beneath. Dollar flung his full length on the brink—hung dangling from the armpits—hung lashing out for the ladder like a boy on a horizontal bar with a mattress just underneath. The top rung took some finding in his reckless haste; and then his hands had to change places with his feet; and it was all a pretty desperate business for no light-weight, in a frenzy of excitement, at the tip-top of a tremulous ladder that leaned against thin air. But his very recklessness saw him down somehow with unbroken bones, and on the threshold of the burning room before the fire had really taken hold. And there he stopped, instead of dashing in; there he stood shrinking from the red light within.

For again one of the women had stayed behind the rest; and through a forest of scaffolding poles, and a swirl of smoke and steam, he beheld her in a glow already dying by her hand, under a hissing stream flung right and left, in glittering coils and spirals, as coolly as a gardener waters the grass. It was his very dream, come true in the end! And Dollar stood there because he was ashamed to look Vera

Moyle in the face—after fearing for one moment that it was nothing but a dream!

But last of all the stream played through the darkness and the smoke, upon the threshold even at his feet, and a dry voice cried:

"I see you all right! I saw you up-stairs; come round and tell me why you ran away."

The little landing was like a gridiron

But it was no moment for going round. He went to her through sparks and splinters in his socks, and felt the pain no more than the relief when he stood beside her on the cool flags of the corridor, with both her hands in his.

"I might have known!" he spluttered through the smoke. "I might have known it even from the first!"

"It's jolly bad luck that you should know it at all," said Lady Vera, in the same dry little voice. "I'm not proud of it, I can tell you."

"Not of stopping an absolutely wanton crime?"

"Not of turning against my old lot—and I haven't, either!" cried Lady Vera, with more passion than he had ever heard from her. "I feel everything I said up-stairs. I think we've all been treated more abominably than ever. I don't blame them a bit for all this sort of thing——"

"Vera, you do—you know you do!"

"I don't; how can I? Haven't I done worse? I may think they're going rather far, and I may put in my spoke——"

"This is not the first time!" he exulted, still only with her hands in his, yet little knowing how he hurt them.

"That's my business," she said, with a sudden laugh that broke her voice. "It's the least I can do—after two years ago."

"And I knew you'd done it!" he was quick to cry. "I knew it hours back, though you did frighten me again just now. I found the hose-pipe in the bathroom with your gloves, and their rotten message rubbed out on the wall! I knew the hose was yours, because I'd just been told there wasn't such a thing in the house. But I was looking for something of the kind. I knew there was something to be found, that the whole thing wasn't what it seemed. And ever since it's been the happiest night of my life, on top of my most miserable hour!"

"I'll motor you back to town for that," said Lady Vera, with another poor little laugh. "I—I'm sorry I didn't tell you this afternoon."

"I'm not!"

"Somehow it didn't seem quite the game by the others, though of course I hoped you would guess that I had only come in after them as a kind of scarecrow. Of course I don't know if it will make you the least bit less miserable——" But there she stuck.

"If what will?"

And now it was she who held his hands the faster—only across a gulf of darkness like a solid wall—only with a kindness that reminded him it was nothing else—only with a glow more dear than an embrace.

"If it makes you the very least bit happier," she whispered, "why, of course it was only just your own game, doctor, that I was trying to play!"

VIII

THE SECOND MURDERER

It was yet another Lady Vera who brought her own sunshine out of the weeping dusk of that October morning. To veil embarrassment on either side, Dollar had switched off the light by which he had just read the line scribbled on her card; but there was no sanction for his nervous sensibility in the little picture he beheld next moment. An audacious study in Venetian red—a tripping fashion-plate with a practical waist—it was only Vera by virtue of the radiant face between the donkey-eared toque and the modish modicum of fur. And though the radiance was lovely as ever in his eyes, and lovelier still as a surprise, this frivolous modernity was pain and puzzledom to Dollar until their hands met, and the one in the tight glove trembled.

"It's no use beating about the bush," said Vera Moyle, and there was no sort of tremor in her voice. "Do you mind telling me exactly what you know of a Mr. Mostyn Scarth?"

"Mostyn Scarth!" cried Dollar. "Do *you* know him?"

"Only too well!"

"I was afraid of it."

"But I want your opinion and experience of him first. I believe you saw something of each other in Switzerland?"

232

"We did," replied Dollar weightily. "He was supposed to be looking after a young temporary lunatic, who was of age, rich, and not irresponsible in the eye of the law. Scarth induced the boy to leave him vast sums of money in a will, and then made two distinct attempts to murder him."

"No!"

"He did. You ask what I know of this man, and I make no bones about telling you. It's a thing the whole world ought to know for its protection. He made two separate attempts on the lad's life, the last more ingenious than the first; first he tried to poison him by means of a forged prescription, and next to break his neck by tampering with his toboggan."

"In Switzerland, when you were there?"

"I was sent for after the first effort; the second was made under my nose."

"And yet you did nothing?"

Lady Vera's indignation was not confined to the absent miscreant; her demigod came in for his share.

"There was not much to be done," he protested humbly. "We were in a foreign country; the evidence wouldn't have been overwhelming under our own law. I let Scarth know that I had found him out, got the boy out of his clutches—pulled *him* together all right—and laid the whole case before Topham Vinson when I came home. He consulted his law officers; they thought I had so little to go upon that our man wasn't even marked down for surveillance by the police. I

233

had to keep my own eye on him when he turned up in town again. Scarth made that easy by immediately getting on my tracks, and discovering in Mr. Croucher another old friend who had his knife in me. They tried between them to pervert my chauffeur; then I lost sight of them; and it was then I wanted to put you on your guard, but you were never in, and my letters seemed to miscarry."

"They didn't," said Lady Vera, with frank contrition. "I am ashamed to tell you why I never answered them; but I will in a minute. So it was Mr. Scarth you meant when you told me the other day that poor Croucher had fallen into such bad hands?"

"Poor Croucher! Yes, it was; and there really is no comparison between them. One was born in the scarlet, so to speak, but the other's the only really educated and quite cold-blooded villain I have ever met."

Vera Moyle sat forward in the patient's chair, in the very attitude of two years before, with the same firelight illumining the same steadfast look of moral and intellectual honesty; and the fuller health upon her cheek, the deeper wisdom in her eyes, made no more difference to Dollar than her superfluous smartness now. She was the same utterly candid creature, about to tell him the whole truth about some fresh trouble, and extenuate nothing that concerned herself.

"I don't want to waste many words on Mr. Scarth," she began, in the least vindictive of human voices; "but I ought to tell you that I quite liked him until the other day. I met him first at a country house where he was supposed to be tutoring the boys, but was really the life and soul of the whole party. It was extraordinary how he ran everything and everybody for those people; we were all devoted to him, and he says I asked him to come and see us in town, but he certainly never came until near the end of this last season. Then he made up for lost time; he's capital company, as you know, and we had him to dinner, and my eldest brother asked him down to stay in August when I was there. That was when we saw most of each other, and Mr. Scarth asked me to marry him——"

"Good God!"

"Of course I didn't like him well enough for that, though he *had* put me against *you*!"

"How?" said Dollar grimly. She was still peering into the fire; but he flattered himself there was more than firelight in the flush that almost rivaled the Venetian red still nearer to the bars.

"He knows what I did two years ago."

"Croucher, of course?"

"He said it was you—that you gave me away to him in Switzerland!"

"And you believed him?"

235

"He made it just credible. He said you told him in confidence; he showed me a letter in which you reminded him not to let it go any further."

"A forgery!"

"I see that now; but it was a very good one, written on your club paper."

"The man's an expert forger. Anybody can go into a club to write a note and steal some stationery. If only you had tackled me about it!"

"I promised I wouldn't. I could hardly believe it of you, all the same—not that you were the first to tell him. But—but it did put me off—in spite of everything—and that was only in July."

"Just when I was trying to see you, to put you on your guard!"

She gave him her eyes at last, and they were wet but beaming. "I doubted it still more from one or two things he said when we had our little scene in the country; but I *knew* there wasn't a word of truth in it before *you* said a dozen words to me the other Sunday! It was all a plot to keep us apart—to get me under his thumb."

"Did he threaten you when you—had your little scene?"

"Not in so many words."

"He will. That's where I shall come in."

"His position was that I and my secret would only be safe with him."

"As it never was with me?"

"That was it; but now he knows that I don't believe him. I told him so when he called last week."

"So you have had another little scene?"

"I cut it short at that."

"And there the matter ended?"

"Between him and me."

"Don't make too sure. You don't know your Mostyn Scarth as well as I do. I wonder what his next move will be!"

The wonder lit the doctor's face with eager interest, but brighter still was the answering light under the toque with the ass's ears of watered silk.

"I don't know about his next, but I can tell you what his latest move is," said Lady Vera. "He has taken to dogging me all over the place, to see if I don't commit another crime! He was one of the alleged detectives at Pax Monktons Chase!"

"Never!" cried Dollar, taken fairly by surprise. He had forgot almost every feature of the affair in question, except how magnificently Vera Moyle had come out of it. The episode remained in his mind only as the one great dream of his that had come true as yet; the details had disappeared like those of any other dream.

"I happen to know it," said Lady Vera, with some little embarrassment. "I had it from—the other detective."

"Not—" and Dollar stopped to frown—"not Croucher himself?"

"Yes."

"He has dared to speak to you!"

"For the very first time since that night in the train; now do listen, and be fair to the poor fellow. He never was as bad as you thought him; you say yourself that he's a saint compared with Mr. Scarth." Dollar was too savage to smile at this free version of what he had said. "Well, they have fallen out, and Croucher's in a bad way altogether; and he has turned to me for a helping hand—not for money or anything of that kind."

"Not the least little hint of blackmail?"

"Not a word or a sign of anything of the sort, except that he asked me to forgive him for the other time, and of course I did."

"Of course you would, though he actually robbed you under arms!" cried Dollar, as sardonically as he felt he must.

But he was let off with the caution of a frown that would have escaped attention on a face less consistently serene than Lady Vera Moyle's.

"You forget what he had been through first," said she, gently. "Within forty-eight hours of execution, for something he had never done! Thinking what he thought, and I neither denied nor admitted, then or at any time, the wonder is not that he behaved as badly as he did that night, but as well as he has ever since. However much you frightened him at the time, he might have gone on blackmailing me without your knowledge, and that's the last thing he's trying to do now. But I want to do something for him! You say yourself that he has fallen into the worst of hands—well, I want to get him out of them. You once told me that, when you had him here before, you found yourself trying to make a decent being of him, and beginning to feel that you might almost succeed. Doctor, I want you to try again, for my sake! He is frightfully sorry for what he did before, and he has been very badly used by Mostyn Scarth. He looks ill. I want you to save his life, and more than his life! He has told me with tears in his eyes that he was never so happy as when you had him here before. Dear man, do take him in again, and give him one more chance, to please me!"

Her voice had broken, and for once her eyes had played her false as well, and Dollar had waited grimly while she recovered her voice or dried her eyes. But he could not answer grimly when in her turn she waited for him to speak. In her frivolous little blazing skirt, in the toque that he liked even less; over-dressy as he dared to think her in his simple heart of hearts, she appealed to him the more profoundly for those very vanities, so far from vanity were the letter and the spirit of her intercession.

"So you really came to see me about Alfred Croucher?" said Dollar, but very gently, without the faintest accent of reproach.

"It was about both of them, but chiefly about him," she admitted. "Of course I wanted to check his account of Mr. Scarth. If you had given him a good character, that would have been the end; but you gave him a much worse one than I expected. Croucher seems almost immaculate by comparison; honestly, I shouldn't wonder if he were less lost to decency through his very association with a man so much worse than himself."

"Did he tell you so?"

"He said it had brought him up with a round turn."

"It's possible," said Dollar, not more dryly than he could help. "The psychology is all right." He was smiling and nodding now. "And where is Mr. Croucher at the moment?"

"Walking up and down outside."

"Until we call him in?"

"If only you will let me!"

She was on her feet, to take him at his word as soon as spoken; but he said that was Barton's job, and, wondering aloud how Barton would like it, went out presumably to see. He was not gone long, and in another minute Alfred Croucher was cringing before them like a beaten cur.

But few curs whine as this one did that morning, while the crime doctor listened and their little lady winced. She was right about one thing. He did look ill; his cough was not altogether put on. He had been "tret somefink crool," he declared, but without entering into particulars, for which Dollar did not press; but on the character of Mostyn Scarth there were no such reservations. Croucher denounced that monster with the white hatred of a holy warrior, casting up his eyes with all manner of passionate and pious invocations.

"Only take me away from 'im, before it's too late!" he implored, reluctant murder in the whites of his rolling eyes. "'E's a bad man, a very bad man 'e is! The 'appiest days o' me life was wot I spent in 'ere eighteen munf ago. It seems more like eighteen years—'ard. I never should've quit but for Shod, wot's got a good long stretch for 'is pines. 'E's another bad man; but for 'im you 'ad me in the 'oller of yer 'and, and might 've made a man o' me in no time."

"Yet you went straight from me to threaten and rob the lady who sent you here!"

It was a dangerous opening, but Croucher did not take it. In ignoble emotion he fell upon the knees of a flash pair of trousers, which still showed the track of an ineradicable crease, and once more sued for the mercy and forgiveness already vouchsafed to him. And Lady Vera turned from the sly, leering, blinking, darting eyes to a pair turned hard as nails, and the harder for an oblique inner twinkle all their own.

"All right!" snapped Dollar, to her intense relief. "I'll take you in, Croucher, for better or worse. Well make it for better, if we can; but do get to your two legs, man, instead of fawning on all four! Are you free to stop as you are, or is there anything you want to settle up first?"

"There's me rooms," said Croucher, eagerly. "There's nuffink worth fetching, but I shouldn't like to bilk the people, 'speshly w'en 'er lidyship's gawn an' give me the money, Gawd bless 'er!"

Dollar precipitated the creature's exit, on the verge of fresh saurian tears, of which there were further signs for his benefit on the mat. He might be a bad man, too, might Mr. Croucher, but he wasn't as bad as Mostyn Scarth. And in that modest claim, at least, there was a bitter sincerity which received its due in a nod of keen acknowledgment.

"I never did think you were more than a second murderer, Croucher!"

"Wot's that?"

The whites of those quick, furtive eyes were showing quite horribly in a moment.

"Only a technical expression, Croucher, meaning the minor malefactor."

And he returned rather slowly into the eager presence of Lady Vera Moyle.

"I suppose I mustn't fawn, either," she said, in the softened tone of one of her rare rebukes. "But—*do* you think you can make anything of him—this time?"

"I hope so; but I shall be very glad to have him back, even if I fail again."

"Why?"

The crime doctor gave her another of his oblique smiles.

"I shall be all the better able to watch Scarth's latest move," he said.

II

Over against the back windows of a nice new street of tall red houses, beyond the high red wall enclosing their common strip of shrubs and gravel, runs a humbler row of windows in connection with a mews. In one you may still catch a coachman shaving for the box, but more likely a chauffeur's lady engrossed in her novelette; and on the next sill are pots of geraniums, while the next but one keeps the evening's kippers nice and fresh. Most of the windows have muslin curtains, and in some the lights are on all night. Last

October there was only one without any kind of covering, except a newspaper stuck across a broken pane.

It was the scandal of the row; a battered billycock lay rotting on the roof above; strange fragments of song were always liable to burst from within, as of a gentleman roistering in his sleep, and at times a bristly countenance would roll red eyes over the backs of the red houses, beginning and ending with the flats at the bottom of the street. If a dark handsome face appeared simultaneously at a top flat window, the chances were that both would vanish, but it would have been difficult to detect the exchange of actual signals.

On the return of Alfred Croucher, shaven and collared, from the audience in Welbeck Street, he went so far as to wink and wave from the window that disgraced the mews to the one that crowned the flats. His rolling eyes still had their whites about them; his wrists were still in unaccustomed cuffs; and Mostyn Scarth was at his elbow before it could be lifted with the bottle brought in to celebrate the occasion.

"Just one!" said Croucher, pitching his mongrel whine in the key of comic extravaganza. "I deserve all ten fingers for what I got to tell yer!"

"Not a drop, my Lazarus!" said Scarth. "When do you move in?"

"To-day—now."

"You shall have the whole bottle when you come out. You may want it. What about that stamped note-paper?"

"Couldn't lay 'ands on a scrap."

"Hadn't you the waiting-room to yourself?"

"My witin'-room was the street, gov'nor."

"Well, I must have a sheet or two as soon as you can stick them in the post; three or four would be safer, and at least a couple of his envelopes, in case of accidents. Now tell me everything that happened; and perhaps you *shall* have a drink before you go."

There was no light that night in the window with the broken pane pasted over with newspaper; next day it was mended properly, and the sodden billycock removed from the roof before Alfred Croucher awoke from his innocent and protracted slumbers in the crime doctor's patent chamber of perpetual peace.

His first impression was that some mysterious miracle had been performed expressly for his behoof. He must have been drunk to have slept so sound, and yet he had none of the disagreeable sensations which a long experience associated with the ordinary orgy. He felt profoundly rested and refreshed; never had he lain in so luxurious a bed; and the air was faintly scented, subtly soothing, and there was plenty of it, yet not a sound except the gentle stirring of his own breathing body between the sheets. His palate was clean and cool beyond belief. He opened his eyes, and saw a plain room sharp as crystal to the sight: not the bronze bedchamber that he suddenly remembered, but the same place steeped in purest sunshine, and ten thousand times fairer for the change.

Then he knew where he was, and precisely why he was there; and it was the mental equivalent of what Mr. Croucher called "'ot coppers," only this made him hot all over. He might have been in a fever; he hoped violently that he was. He remembered his cough, and began to practise it. A determined paroxysm revived his spirits; he was not fit to get up, and other people would just have to wait until he was, and serve 'em jolly well right!

Other people couldn't get at him there; yet one other person could, and did, to Mr. Croucher's mingled discomfort and relief. The doctor duly kept him in bed; but there was too much of the doctor; and yet the time hung heaviest when he was not there, and there were heavier burdens even than the time. The patient had lost his liking for a book. Conversation was more to his taste this time. His mind would wander when he read. It would follow the doctor down-stairs to his consulting-room, or across the landing to the room in which he slept. The man haunted him; it was better to have him there in the flesh, than to see him as Croucher continually saw him when he was not there at all.

Better, again, to talk of some things than to dwell on them night and day, especially when those subjects seemed to possess an equally awful fascination for the crime doctor. Of course, they were in his line; that accounted for the doctor's

246

morbid taste, and the patient's most terrible experience was quite enough to account for his. There was nothing unnatural in their talks. They had the thing in common, only from opposite poles of experience, which enormously enhanced the mutual interest. If there was one subject they were bound to have discussed, with no false delicacy on either side, each being what he was, it was the subject of the sixth commandment.

"Of course you think about it," said Dollar, dismissing an incoherent excuse on the second day. "It must haunt you; it's only natural that it should. All I should like you to do, since you never committed one, and are the last man in the world to commit one now, is to take a rather lighter view of that particular misdeed."

"A lighter view!" repeated Croucher, goggling; and he added with a shuddering inconsequence: "The lor o' the land don't make light of it!"

"Literature has been known to," rejoined the doctor, with as little apparent point. "But you are not the reader you were last year; otherwise there's a little thing, *On Murder Considered as One of the Fine Arts*, that I should like to lend you."

"One o' the 'ow much?" said Mr. Croucher, uncertain whether to grin, or frown, and meanwhile glaring more than he supposed.

Dollar went for the book, and read a few extracts aloud. They appeared to afford him extraordinary enjoyment; they were altogether over the bullet head on the pillow. Croucher could only gather that some people seemed to imagine it was good sport to commit a murder. Funny fools! Let them try a fortnight in the condemned cell, for one they never did commit, and see how they took to that!

But he could understand them that knew nothing about it writing a lot of rot like this; what beat him was that the crime doctor, of all people, and with all his uncanny knowledge of the subject, that even he was able to view the worst of crimes in a light which would never have dawned on the independent intellect of Alfred Croucher. It seemed to him a more lurid light than any in which he himself, at his worst, had ever seen such things; horrible, to his mind, that one who ran every risk of being murdered should sit there gloating over "the shades of merit" in one murder, and over others as "the sublimest and most entire in their excellence that ever were committed." What was more horrible, however, was the hollow note of Mr. Croucher's own laughter, and the furtive gleaming of his restless eyes, while his body twitched between the sheets.

He asked for the book when Dollar rose to go; and was discovered, in due course, bathed in a perspiration which he made less effort to conceal.

"It ain't all like them funny bits," he assured the doctor, with an open shudder. "There's a bit I struck about a servant gal, on one side of a door, an' a bloke wot's done the 'ole bloomin' family in on the other. My cripes! I 'ad to 'old me breff over that, and it's made me sweat like a pig."

"On which side of the door were you?"

"Wot's that?"

"In your mind's eye, my good fellow!"

Mr. Croucher had seldom found it easier to tell the truth, and he made the most of his opportunity.

"I felt as if I was the gal," said he. "Shouldn't wonder if I dreamt I was 'er to-night!"

"Ah! I always find myself on the inside," said Dollar, with extraordinary gusto. "I'd much rather have been the girl. She had the open street behind her, and the street-lamps; he had only his own handiwork in the dark, and hardly room enough to step out of the way of it. She got away, too, whereas he had to make away with himself. But I always would rather be the victim; he doesn't know what's coming; and it's not a thousandth part as bad as—the other thing—when it does come.... I'm sorry, Croucher! You shouldn't have asked me to leave you the book; but there's nothing like looking at a thing from all sides, and it may console you to know that you've perspired over the best description of a murder ever written."

Yet that was not the last of their morbid conversations; they would hardly be five minutes together before the noxious subject would crop up, nearly always through some reluctant yet irresistible allusion on the patient's part. The doctor might come in overflowing with deliberate gaiety; there was something about him that set the bulbous eyes rolling with uneasy cunning, the cockney tongue wagging in its solitary strain, as it were under protest from the beaded brow.

On one occasion Dollar was the prime offender. It was the day after Croucher's introduction to De Quincey and the first bad night spent by anybody in the Chamber of Peace. He declared he had not slept a wink, and was advised to get up and go for a walk.

"Alone?" said Croucher in a low voice.

"Why not? This isn't prison, and I never hear you cough. *You* are not going to die just yet, Croucher!"

"I 'ope nobody is, not 'ere," said Croucher, with a horrid twitch. "I feel as it *might* buck me up—a breff of air on a nice fine day like this." His eyes rolled undecidedly, and the oil ran out of his voice. "But it ain't no fun goin' out alone."

"Haven't you any friends you could go and see?"

"No!" cried Croucher, with an emphasis that pulled him up. "I—I might write a letter, though—if you could spare me a bit o' paper wiv the address."

It was a very short letter that Alfred Croucher wrote, but a remarkably thick envelope that he himself took to the post, after looking many times up and down the street. And at the pillar-box, which was not many yards from the door, he again hesitated sadly before thrusting it in.

In the afternoon Dollar took him out in the car, and then it was that for once the poisonous topic was not introduced by Mr. Croucher.

"See that house?" said Dollar, pointing out one of the most modest in the purlieus of Park Lane. "There was no end of a murder *there* once. Swiss valet cut his master's throat, made what he flattered himself were the hall-marks of burglars, and had the nerve to go into the room to wake the dead man up next morning."

"Fair swine, eh?" said Mr. Croucher, with all the symptoms of disgust.

"A very fair artist, too," rejoined the disciple of De Quincey. "That wasn't his only good touch. He cut the old gentleman's throat from ear to ear, and yet there wasn't a spot of blood on his garments. How do you suppose he managed that? It's a messy operation, Croucher; you or I would have made a walking shambles of ourselves!"

"How did he manage it?" asked Croucher, in a shaky growl.

"By taking off every stitch before he did the trick. How about that for a tip?"

251

Croucher made no reply. His teeth were clenched like those of a man bearing physical pain. They were nearly out of town, and Dollar had discoursed upon autumn tints and the nip in the air before being abruptly interrogated as to the "fair swine's" fate.

"Need you ask?" said he. "The poor devil was too clever by half, and made a big mistake for each of his strokes of genius. He was taken, tried, condemned, and all the rest of it! And a greater writer than the gentleman who kept you awake last night wrote the best description of—all the rest of it—in existence. But don't you ask me to lend you that!"

"They always seem to forget somefink," said Alfred Croucher, another long mile out of town.

"The first thing being that the best murders oughtn't to look like murders," the criminologist agreed. "They ought to look like accidents, or suicides at the most. But it takes a Mostyn Scarth to cut as deep as that."

"Wot the 'ell mikes yer fink of 'im?" cried Croucher, in a fury at the very name.

"Well, among other things, the fact that he saw us off in the car just now. Do you mean to say you didn't see through the false beard of the gentleman who was picking up his umbrella as we turned into Wigmore Street?"

III

Never again did Alfred Croucher venture out alone, even as far as the pillar-box; not another letter had he to post, though he received one, wrapped round a stone, once when his window was open, and literally devoured every word. He did go out, but only with the crime doctor in his car, for an hour or two in the afternoon.

More than once they got out at Richmond Park, sent the car across to one of the other gates, and followed at a brisk walk, shoulder to shoulder, with Croucher often peeping over his, but Dollar never. The walk was sometimes broken for as long as it took Croucher to smoke a pipe in one or another of the beautiful wooded enclosures which are the inner glory of the most glorious of all public parks. There, under red canopies of dying leaves, their feet upon a russet carpet of the dead, the smoker would rest in a restless silence, because the one subject which had made him eloquent was now tabooed. Even in the Chamber of Peace there was no peace for Alfred Croucher, and but little sleep, although the doctor had walked him off his legs and would sit beside him till all hours. So the literary and conversational treatment had been altered once for all; and now the patient would hardly read or speak a word.

Late one night, in the second half of the month, the crime doctor, seated like a waxwork in a chair that never creaked, had just made sure that his man was asleep at last. He decided to steal out and write some letters, and take them to the post himself before locking up; and was getting by inches to his catlike feet, when some sense held him bent like a bow. It could hardly have been his hearing, in his own sound-proof sanctuary between double windows and triple doors. Yet suddenly he was all on edge, listening with nerves laid bare by forced vigils in that slumberous room, brown as an Arab in its weird lighting; the silver patch in his hair changed from a florin to a new penny, the whites of his eyes like broad gold rings; their one flaw augmented by an infinite fatigue, their one care the human wreckage on the bed—shattered utterly by him, to be by him built up afresh, but not in the midst of excursions and alarms. And here was the inmost door opening, so softly, so slowly, at deadliest dead of night!

It was a woman who entered like a ghost, and he knew her step, though he could not hear it even now. And though her cloak and head-dress were those of a trained nurse, he knew, rather than saw, that the wearer was Lady Vera Moyle.

"Hush!" she was the first to whisper, and very softly closed the last door, through which he would have hurried her out again. Already her soundless movements, her air of vast precaution, puzzled him even more than her presence or her dress; but he still had anxieties on this side of the door.

"Just asleep," he whispered, pointing to the bed. "Bad time I've given him, poor brute, but a better one coming, I do believe. Did you come to see how he was doing?" Even in the stained light she looked so beaming now, so frankly triumphant, he made sure that was it. "I'd have written, but thought you were away. Who let you in?"

"This!"

And she held up a new Yale key.

"Where did you get it?"

"Specially cut for me." Every line in his red man's face was a note of blank interrogation. "Mostyn Scarth has another—cut specially for him! I've had him watched."

"Vera!"

"*I* was watching *for* him—from the nursing home opposite—suffrage friends of mine."

"Why didn't you tell me?"

"You had enough to do."

He shook his head. "Well?"

"He's somewhere in the house."

"This house?"

"Why didn't you tell me?"

She nodded. "Hiding—in your room, I think."

"I'll soon have him out!"

"Wait!" She had eyes for the amber bed at last. "Are you sure he's asleep?"

Dollar stole across and back. The great frame was breathing gently and evenly as a child. "But he's a terribly light sleeper; we mustn't disturb him, if we can help it."

"Disturb him!" She clutched his hand for the first time. "I wish to God I had never brought him to you! There's a plot between them, doctor—I know there's some plot!"

"There *was*, of course," he said, smiling, but wincing at his own "of course" that instant. "I'm delighted you brought him," he reassured her. "I've taken some of the plot out of him—and now for Mr. Scarth!"

He reached past her to open the door. In a flash she put something in his hand. It was a showy little revolver, the handle mother-of-pearl, the barrel golden in that light.

"Thanks," he said-briefly—but there was a whole novel in his look. "Now will you do something more for me?"

"No!" she said flatly, and was at his elbow when he opened his own door across the landing.

It was such a plain little room that there was indeed small danger of a surprise from the concealed intruder. The only possible cover was under the bed, behind the curtains, or in the wardrobe. Dollar just went through the form of glancing under the bed, as he whipped up the poker in his left hand; with it he parted the curtains, and in the same second had his man comfortably covered at arm's length.

"Well done!" cried the girl.

Scarth repaid her with a gleam of saturnine enlightenment; it was the first change in his swarthy, unemotional, unconquerable visage. On the Balkan battle-fields there may have been myriads of such faces, not with the unique intellectual quality of this one, but alike in their fierce contempt of battle, murder, and sudden death, as little matters not worth a qualm, whether in the active or the passive party to the business. Among educated Englishmen the temperament is rare, and rarer still the mental attitude; in the combination lie the makings of the hell-born villain, and Mostyn Scarth was the finished article.

Stoical in his discomfiture, he saw his opening with no more than a glitter of his insolent eyes, and took it as though he had never foreseen anything else.

"So I've caught you both out, my virtuous friends!" said he. "And you dare to present that thing at me, as though I were here for a felonious purpose!"

"I shall not empty it into you, Scarth, however much you may tempt me," replied the crime doctor. "What do you say to clasping both hands behind your head and leading the way down-stairs?"

"I'll see you damned first," said Mostyn Scarth.

"Good! It's exactly the same to me, only you may find it harder not to take one of those hands out of your trousers pockets, and the moment you show a finger I shall cripple you for life. I thought, too, that you might like to hear what we say to the police."

"I don't take the faintest interest in what *you* say to them," returned Scarth, with a broader gleam to light his meaning.

"Good again! Do you mind going down and ringing up New Scotland Yard, Lady Vera? On your way you might please see if all three doors are shut in the room opposite; then, perhaps—no! I should leave this one open after all, I think." Three seconds had sufficed to close the triple doors, one more quickly than another, behind them.

"I should, if I were you," said Scarth. "And I should think a good many times before carrying out your other instructions—if I were the lady at the bottom of one of the few mysteries that still puzzle Scotland Yard."

There was a pause, in which Dollar heard only a sharp intake of breath on the threshold just behind him; but that was enough.

"I believe I shall have to shoot you, after all," said he, and the hammer of the mother-of-pearl revolver clicked to full cock.

"Won't that rather spoil your game?" said Scarth, blandly.

"Mine is not the game that matters at the moment—yours *is*. As, however, you have been fool enough to have a key cut expressly to fit my front-door lock, and have been discovered in my room at midnight——"

"In the most distinguished company! Go on, Dollar. Nothing extenuate—bang the field-piece—twang the lyre!"

His teeth were showing as they had shown on the platform at Winterwald nine months before; the tag from his famous impersonation had slipped out with all the snap and gusto which had captivated an unruly audience then; and it was not without a slight mesmeric effect on the man who had him at his mercy. If Scarth in turn had not held Vera Moyle at *his* mercy, and if John Dollar had not known him to be utterly devoid of that quality, he could have admired the cool daredevil, swaggering at bay.

"Remember the concert at Winterwald, doctor," he went on, "and our talk afterward, and the last talk we ever had there? He thought I had two tries to kill a fellow, Lady Vera—two bites at such a green young nut! Better to finish 'em off at one fell blow, isn't it? Not such fun for the widow, or the poor innocent devil who nearly swings for the job, but great work for the militant Millies and their lady leader! Splendid for you all until the truth comes out—as it will the minute a policeman shows his nose!"

It was Lady Vera who had obtained him this hearing. She had stepped up to Dollar, had taken his arm, had even put her other hand in front of her own revolver.

"Let him go on; we may as well know where we are," she had said in the middle of Scarth's speech. And now she asked him what he proposed, as if she were inquiring the price of a dress, with the civility doubly due to an inferior.

"You have had my proposal," said Scarth. "It's not the kind that one repeats before a third party."

"I may as well ring them up," said Lady Vera, trying to disengage her arm; but Dollar's had closed upon it, and his left hand held hers as in a vise.

"You shan't!" he ground out. "It's all bluff. They have no evidence."

"They are welcome to all I can give them," she answered. "I have always regretted I didn't come forward in the beginning. But there was more excuse than there is now—then there was no question of letting a worse person go for the second time."

But this was not said for the worse person's benefit; for the Vera Moyles it is impossible to speak *at* the worst person in the world. The point was merely urged as an argument for Dollar's private ear. But the Mostyn Scarths are expert listeners; not a syllable was lost upon the consummate chieftain of that foul family; and he grinned gaily through as much of the open door as he could see from this point.

"So you admit that you administered his coup de grace to the late lamented Sergeant Simpkins?"

But the heavy shaft was not winged by one of Mostyn Scarth's feathered glances. His grinning gaze still sped past them to the landing.

"I have never denied it in my life."

"Hear that, Croucher?" cried Scarth. "'Full confession by Lady Vera Moyle—extry spechul.'"

The pair stood closer as one of them looked round; and there, indeed, on the threshold, bulked Alfred Croucher, larger than life in a white bathgown that sat better on him than his loudest clothes. And his unwholesome face looked only a shade less white than all the rest of him, but for the little red sleepless eyes fixed on Mostyn Scarth, who still enjoyed the crime doctor's undivided attention.

"'Ow the 'ell did *you* get 'ere?" said Croucher huskily.

"I'm obliged to you for asking. Our virtuous friends are so ready to take a felony for granted, that it seems never to have occurred to them that I walked in at the door—partly to see you—chiefly to bowl them out." Lady Vera could not help smiling at that which seemed never to have occurred to her; nothing else left any mark, save upon John Dollar, on whom Scarth now trained his ivory grin. "The worst of a Yale lock, doctor," he went on, "is that all the keys are numbered; the worst of a Turkish bath is that your enemy may do that thing, and have a look at your latch-key if you will leave it in your pocket on its chain. Northumberland Avenue may be a good place after a bad night, but that's where I really found my way into your house. You didn't see me because I had the bad taste to prefer the cave of electricity to the public hot-rooms and your capital company."

The note of insolence had been forced for Croucher's benefit, the libretto elaborated to impress that elemental mind, and it was to Croucher that Scarth turned for applause. It might have been more articulate; there was little merriment in the guttural laugh; and it was not in open mockery, if not with any visible respect, that the little red eyes sought the silent object of these insults.

Dollar met them for a moment with a sidelong flash; that was as much as the little red eyes could stand. Scarth glowered, but Mr. Croucher was not looking up any more. Between the two strong men, one spitting insults with his tongue, the other darting questions with his eyes, flabby Croucher found it convenient to study the toes of his bedroom slippers. But his right hand shook deep in the far pocket of the voluminous bathgown. None of them saw that but Mostyn Scarth, and him it filled with gleaming confidence.

"Come, Alfred," said he, "get into your street clothes, if they haven't been taken away from you. If they have, go down as you are and call a taxi. I'm going to take you out of this hole. You look more dead than alive. I thought you might; that's one reason why I came."

"Croucher is going to do something for me first," said the crime doctor. "*Then* he can do what he likes."

"Sorry you haven't got a soul to call your own, Alfred."

"Who says I haven't?"

"Doctor Dollar. Didn't you hear him?"

"If he does, he's a———"

"Croucher! Croucher!" said the doctor. "All I want you to do is to hand me the razor case from the dressing-table. In fact you needn't do all that; just arm yourself with the weapon you ought to find there. Then somebody will be more of a match for me. And Mr. Scarth isn't raising any further objection, you will notice."

What Croucher noticed, as the red eyes came up at last, was that Mostyn Scarth had suddenly lost a little of his usual healthy tan; but the bedroom slippers remained planted where they were.

And then without a word Lady Vera stepped from the doctor's side, took the razor-case in both her hands, pulled it in two and exhibited the empty halves.

"Which of you has borrowed my razor?" said John Dollar.

"Not *me*!" cried Croucher with tremendous emphasis. But his right hand was still in his far pocket, as only Mostyn Scarth could see; and the sight restored a little of that healthy tan which so becomes dark faces.

"Not you, Croucher?"

"No, not me, by Gawd!"

"Yet I believe your original mission in this house was to possess yourself of that razor—and—use it?"

Dollar did not finish the sentence without feeling for a little hand with his left; that little hand met it half-way, and was the first to give a reassuring squeeze.

"You were to do something to me with it, I believe, and to leave it in my hand to show I'd done it myself?"

And then, under another sidelong flash, that steadied down into a will-destroying gleam, Croucher came out with a dreadful phrase.

"To guide yer 'and!" said he, hoarsely.

"To guide my hand! Exactly! But it was not exactly your idea?"

"No. It was——"

But here his eyes rolled into Mostyn Scarth's, and dropped once more.

"Exactly!" repeated Dollar. "But you didn't quite feel like doing it, so at last your master had to come in to do it for you?"

"He ain't my master now, blast 'im!"

"Steady, Croucher. May I ask what that is in your hand?"

It was a letter. Only a letter out of that far pocket, after all! Scarth's eyes started, and he found his tongue once more.

"You—give—that—to me, Croucher!"

Croucher wavered at his voice; it was terribly threatening, each subtle tone a poisoned barb.

"What if I don't?"

"You know what!"

"The game deepens," said the crime doctor; and he did not know that his left hand had dropped the hand of hands for him.

"*Your* game's up if you show that letter!" cried Scarth to Croucher, who only showed him the broad of his back.

"Can you be tried twice for the same thing, doctor?" he began—but in the same breath he desperately added: "I don't care whether you can or you can't! You read that, whether or no!"

The letter was in an envelope superscribed "To the Coroner," in a wonderful imitation of Dollar's handwriting; but the letter itself, written on his own stamped paper, was a still more marvelous forgery, in which the crime doctor bade farewell to the world before stultifying his own life's work by the crime of suicide.

"That's better than anything you did in Switzerland," said Dollar, nodding to the livid man between the curtains.

"But it ain't the best thing 'e's done," cried Croucher, and stopped to roll his eyes and gloat. "The bounder's best bit was squeezin' two people for the same job—the guilty an' the innercent—'er as thought she must 've done it, an' 'im as knew 'e done it all the time!"

"That's the end of *you*," said Scarth, with sardonic satisfaction.

"It's the beginning of us all!" said the crime doctor, in a voice they hardly knew. "Do you—can you mean yourself and this lady?"

That lady shook her head and smiled.

"I do, if I swing to-morrow!" swore Alfred Croucher. "I told '*im*"—with a truculent thrust of the bullet head—"one night in me cups; an' fust 'e starts squeezin' 'er to marry 'im, an' then squeezin' me to do yer in before yer forbids 'is banns! Oh, 'e's a nut, I tell yer—though we've been the nuts an' 'im the cracker!"

Lady Vera looked like a little ghost, still unable to believe her ears, still staring into space as if the trouble were rather with those great Irish eyes of hers.

But the doctor was the doctor an instant longer. His left hand went out to his patient first.

"You'll sleep to-night! I'll give you the other when it's free," he said, still covering the man with his hands in his pockets, the curtains on each side of him, and a back window just behind.

Then two things happened in quick succession; but the first brought the lover back to life with such a throb that the second was not even seen.

Just saying, "I'm afraid I'm going to make a fool of myself," all that he loved on earth collapsed at his feet. The doctor was down on his knees beside her, getting the girl into his arms. And even Mr. Croucher did not see the curtains close, or hear anything happen behind them; for he, too, was on his knees, holding out a dripping sponge, and babbling faster than the drops pattered on the floor.

"It's right! I done it ... that pore copper in the fog! She sent 'im reelin'—into me arms—but I done all the rest. Never meant to, mind yer, but that's neither here nor there. Ready to swing, I was, an' don't care now if I do! She saved me—little knock-out—an' look 'ow I went an' tret 'er for it!... Gawd, doctor, wot a fair swine I was!"

But the crime doctor had even less time to listen to him now; for the eyes of eyes had opened, were gazing up into his; and not one of them had heard the window raised behind the curtains, or the clanging thud upon the iron steps just underneath.

THE END